THE NEXT WORLD

*To Rosemary
with Best Wishes
Love,
Gene*

THE NEXT WORLD

Gratton E. Coffman

Caster Enterprises
Sun Prairie, Wisconsin

Caster Enterprises

The Next World

All rights reserved.

Copyright © 1997 Gratton E. Coffman

Reproduction in any manner, in whole or in part,
in English or in other languages, or otherwise
without written permission of the copyright holder
is prohibited.

This is a work of fiction. In some instances,
actual people or events are mentioned to lend
versimlitude. All other characters and events
portrayed in this book are fictional, and any
resemblance to real people or incidents
is purely coincidental.

For information, address Caster Enterprises,
3625 Heatherstone Ridge, Sun Prairie, Wisconsin 53590.

PRINTING HISTORY
First Printing 1997

ISBN: 0-9655-206-1-7

PRINTED IN THE UNITED STATES OF AMERICA

10 9 8 7 6 5 4 3 2 1

Acknowledgments

The author extends his thanks to the University of Michigan Athletic Department, The Northwestern University Department of Athletics and Recreation, and the University of Wisconsin Athletic Department. He also especially thanks Jim Bakken, Jim Mott and Thom Strauss.

Author's Notes

The events described as having followed the Wisconsin-Michigan football game on October 30, 1996 actually happened. In fact, the author attended the game and watched the near tragedy unfold. All of the Badger players mentioned were among those involved in the rescue efforts.

And, yes, a man named C.M. Hollister was, indeed, the Northwestern University football coach from 1899 through 1902.

For Dreamers Everywhere

Chapter 1

1933

Arthur Hollister rubbed his eyes and looked around him. What he beheld both fascinated and puzzled him. The puzzlement was destined to fade over time, but never the fascination.

Hollister's last memory had him in the living room of his gracious Evanston home, sitting on the sofa with his arms wrapped tightly around his beloved Amy Lawrence. It was the evening of October 6, 1933, and a few minutes earlier the two of them had bid farewell to David Curtis, a young man who had convinced Hollister that he, Curtis, was a time traveler from 1976, who had ventured back to 1933 to seek his fortune.

Young Curtis had warned them that the house they occupied would explode into flames that very evening, killing them both if they remained inside. Knowing they were both victims of incurable cancer, with but a short time to live anyway, Art and Amy had opted to simply await their collective fates.

Now Hollister found himself in a large hall, surrounded by hundreds of others. The first thing Hollister noted was that everyone appeared to be naked, and that everyone was the same color, sort of a beige. Massive signs on various walls all said the same thing:

> *Welcome to the Main Receiving Area. At your leisure, please proceed to one of the orientation rooms and be seated.*

Making his way to a nearby doorway, Hollister entered a room not unlike a modern and comfortable auditorium. The room filled in a short time, the doors closed and the houselights dimmed. A figure approached the podium, and addressed the group.

"Good morning, everyone, and welcome to orientation. I'm Marla, and I'll be your host during this part of your processing. After I've touched on a few points, we'll all watch a movie which will, hopefully, answer more questions for you than it raises. When the film is over, we'll have an open question and answer period before you all move on to the next stage.

"As I'm sure you have all gathered by now, yes, we are all dead. All you newcomers are in the Naked Soul phase of things. We who are currently serving with the processing staff are well beyond that stage, but when we appear before you we're just as bare and boring looking as you are.

"Before you got here, right after you died, you all went through a step called 'Initial Sort and Selection.' The vast majority always makes it through, but the absolutely lowest types, the mass murderers, other complete slime and hopeless cases, are eliminated.

"We don't operate a heaven or hell. There's no place where angelic choirs fill the air with resounding song, no one sits on clouds playing harps, and great mobs of people don't find themselves bored out of what is left of their minds. On the opposite side of things, no souls find themselves enduring perpetual torment, either. In brief, no one has a thing to fear about dying.

"What we do operate here is a vast rooming house complex. In due time you'll all be given the opportunity to reside in the complex, and to participate in such options as you may select from the many which are available. And now, let's watch the movie."

For the next 30 minutes, Hollister and the rest viewed a full-color sound presentation that explained a lot of what was to come for them, and generally put their minds at ease. After the movie, the houselights came back up, and Marla's assistants passed out guidebooks to everyone. Each guidebook had a location and time indicated, during which the newcomer was supposed to report for his or her personal placement interview. Each guidebook also included a detachable questionnaire and a pencil, so that the interviewee could fill in the blanks before the appointment.

Hollister took time to fill out his questionnaire and then, halfway down a long corridor, he found his appointed interview room, and was ushered in by a receptionist. As the interviewer closed the door, he and Hollister underwent instant transformation.

Both were now dressed as businessmen, and Hollister could tell by his reflection in a conveniently placed mirror that he himself appeared to be in his early thirties, and in the prime of health. The man he faced across the desk seemed about the same age, and Hollister felt instantly at ease with him. The interviewer introduced himself as Jothan Edwards, and welcomed Hollister to TNW, short, as he explained, for The Next World.

"Okay, Joe," Hollister said, handing Edwards the filled-in questionnaire, "now please tell me what this is all about, what I can expect, and what options I have. By the way, please call me Art."

"Fair enough, Art. It's refreshing to meet someone like you. I somehow feel that had we met, once upon a time, in the real life business world, we'd have gotten along just fine.

"So, as one former businessman to another, here's the deal. Your options are, essentially, two. You can volunteer for immediate re-cycling into the body of a baby about to be born, then wait to grow up and see how that lifetime works out. Or, you can go into our rooming house program, which already offers a number of opportunities, with more being added all the time."

"Which route would you take, Joe, if you were in my shoes?"

"Tell you what, Art, let's take a look at the record. Generally speaking, information on a soul's past lives is screened off from him, except for the last one. But just once each cycle, at the entry interview, an individual gets a chance to peek into the past a bit."

Wheeling his desk chair back to the wall behind his desk, Edwards slid a wall panel aside, reached into the rather large opening it revealed, and exposed a piece of equipment which, to the eyes of a 1990's businessman, would look remarkably like a desktop personal computer. Flipping the ON switch, Edwards waited a short while, then typed in a few key strokes. The display screen filled with data, and with a grin Edwards beckoned Hollister over to take a look.

"All you remember now," Edwards began, "and all you'll remember once you leave this office, is your just completed life. During that one you became a motion picture director, then switched career directions and established a large and successful plumbing supply

THE NEXT WORLD 5

manufacturing plant. You were too old for active military service during the World War, but your firm made tremendous contributions to the war production effort. You never married, but during your later years you had a long and loving relationship with a lady named Amy Lawrence. You died at age 59, a happy multi-millionaire.

"Now, let's see what else you've done over the years—at least let's look at a few of your past careers. As a British naval officer, you chased down Pirates in the Caribbean; you had a brief but exciting life as a stockman on an Australian cattle station; as a Major General in the Union Army you commanded an infantry Corps during the Civil War, even though such a command usually called for a Lieutenant General, the rank you held when you were killed in action, just before the end of the war. It looks like the only reason you didn't put in a stint playing piano in a New Orleans bordello is that you never could find the time in between your other careers. Offhand, Art, I'd say it's time you gave it a rest for a while!"

"When you put it that way, Joe, perhaps you're right. Now, tell me about this rooming house program."

Chapter 2

Roughly half an hour later, as Hollister left Jothan Edwards' office, his business suit attire disappeared, and he was once again a naked soul among other naked souls. Somehow being nude didn't bother him half as much as the blah beige color of his skin, hair, eyes and every part of him. Although he never stubbed a toe or in any way injured himself, it also bothered Hollister that he had no shoes to wear.

At any rate, Edwards' answers about the rooming house program had been satisfactory enough to entice Hollister into signing up for it. Safely tucked into a pocket of Hollister's Guidebook was his newly-issued All Purpose Card, which would serve as Hollister's ID, his ultrasonic transport card, his quick-connect telephone card and his door key.

Since he had all the time he would ever need, and no pressure to be anywhere at any specific hour, Hollister decided to find a place to relax and assimilate everything he had learned so far. This decision made, it seemed almost no time before Art found an inviting lounge area, with plenty of available and comfortable-looking seating available. Taking a seat, Hollister leaned back and began to re-cap what he had already learned from the orientation movie, the interview with Jothan Edwards, a perusal of his guide book and his own powers of observation.

"So," Hollister mused, "what do we know so far?"

"Here we all are in The Next World, and here we will all stay until such time as we opt to recycle into a new living body on Earth. Each of us here retains the identity he or she had in his or her most recent life. The identity, yes, and much of the personality, but none of the misery.

"The Wonderful Central Processor eliminates from each soul's make-up those traits which simply have no place here, such as jealousy, cruelty and greed. Crime simply does not exist. There is one common language, no religion, no politics, no money, no disease or personal injuries, and in all public situations there is no variance in skin color.

"Regardless of people's age or physical condition at the time of their death back on Earth, here in The Next World they are all in their prime. In privacy, when they take on a human appearance, most souls appear to be in their mid-twenties to early thirties. They look as they did at that stage in their previous lives, or as they would have appeared had they reached that stage in life unscathed by accident, disease or other disfigurement. No one is physically or mentally handicapped. Some are beautiful or handsome, many are quite attractive, the majority are average looking, and no one is cursed by unbearable ugliness.

"Each rooming unit is occupied by 16 tenants on a more or less permanent basis, and each unit has accommodations for up to 4 guests at any one time. In effect, the occupants of each unit become a family. The Wonderful Central Processor selects the members of each dwelling unit on the basis of their potential compatibility with each other. By no means does this mean a cookie cutter sameness is the result. Although an individual's desire to move to a different unit is an extremely rare occurrence, the system does provide for such a process, just as it does for supplying a replacement for a soul who opts for recycling somewhere along the line.

"As the old expression goes, I'm sure this is just the tip of the iceberg. But, after all, we've all got until forever to discover the subtle nuances."

On his way into the lounge Hollister had passed a Travel Station, and he now arose and walked over to it. Extracting his All Purpose Card from his guide book, Hollister inserted the card in the slot marked "Travel." The screen in front of him immediately displayed a message: "Thank you, Mr. Hollister. Please remove your card, then push a lettered button corresponding to your desired destination."

On the console, only the "A" button, labeled "Home" was illuminated as a potential choice. So, Hollister pushed the "A" button.

Seemingly only moments later, Hollister found himself standing at another Travel Station, this one just outside a tall, wide apartment building, on what appeared to be an endless street lined with such buildings. Every building Hollister could see was painted differently. This one was bright yellow, with white dazzle stripes. The number on the door read KK 280. Hollister once again got out his All Purpose Card, inserted it in the door's card slot, and withdrew it again. The door swung open, Hollister entered, and the door closed behind him.

To Hollister's surprise, the moment the outside door clicked shut he became clothed again, this time in slacks, sweater, casual sox and shoes. Apparently, once a tenant was inside his own building he was no longer considered to be out in public, and his appearance once again became "human."

Hollister spotted a reception desk in the lobby, approached it, then stopped and stared at the lady behind the counter. She was an attractive, long haired brunette, well put together, and dressed in a chic deep blue business suit, complete with a frilly white blouse or dickey, Hollister couldn't tell which. The lady wore just the right amount of cosmetics, a pendant necklace and a very pleasant scent as well. Seldom at a loss for words, Hollister stood there like a tongue-tied, gawking school boy.

The lady looked up, smiled, and inquired "May I help you, sir?"

Hollister, finally remembering his manners, replied. "Yes, please, I do need some directions, but first I want to apologize for staring at you. You're the first pretty lady I've seen since I've been here in The Next World. In fact, not counting naked souls and one receptionist, you're the first lady I've seen at all!"

"That's quite all right, sir. I certainly don't take any offense, and I can understand your reaction. Truth to tell, it happens quite a lot. Now, how can I help you?"

"Well, as I said, I'm new here. I guess what I need is my rooming unit assignment, and directions on how to get there. Here's my All Purpose Card."

The receptionist took the card, inserted it into a slot in the machine on her desk, and pushed a button. Seconds later a slip of paper printed out. The lady took the paper, glanced at it, then handed the paper and card back to Hollister.

"You're in Unit 414, Mr. Hollister. Just take the elevator to the fourth floor and turn right. And, welcome to Building KK 280. We'll probably run into each other on the pool terrace one of these evenings during happy hour!"

The lady behind the desk turned to help another new arrival, and as Hollister walked to the nearby elevator, he smiled to himself. Somehow he knew he was going to like it here!

Chapter 3

At Unit 414, Hollister slipped his card in the key slot, withdrew it, pushed open the door and walked in. No sooner had Hollister closed the door behind him than he was confronted by an attractive and businesslike blonde woman, who appeared to be about 30. The lady was carrying a clipboard.

 Good afternoon, sir," said the lady. "I'm Sandra Richards, and you are?"

"Art Hollister, ma'am. My card opened the door, so I think I'm in the right place."

Miss Richards consulted her clipboard briefly, then replied, "Absolutely right, Mr. Hollister. You're in Room 8, and you make the seventh one to report in."

"And you, Miss Richards, are you one of the permanent group here in Unit 414?"

"No, Mr. Hollister, I'm staying here in one of the guest rooms until I help you all get organized and functioning smoothly. Then I'll be moving on to another new unit. I've always enjoyed meeting new people, and in this work I get to know a lot of them."

"You call what you do 'work'. Does that mean you are compensated for your efforts?"

"Those of us who fill all of the job slots here in The Next World do so on a volunteer basis. We work when we want to work, and relax when we want to do that. Our compensation is in the satisfaction we derive from helping others. I'll be here for a month or so, and before I leave we'll have lots of time to visit and talk, both as a group and on a one-on-one basis. Right now I see that someone else has come in, so I'll leave you on your own for a while, to look around the place and get settled into your room."

Thanking the lady, Hollister wandered over to a wall there in the vestibule, on which several floor plans were displayed. The first illustration was labeled *First Floor Offices and Common Areas*. The layout included the now familiar ground floor reception area, various offices and conference rooms, several large meeting rooms, gymnasiums, work shops, theaters, a library and miscellaneous other spaces. It appeared that each floor of the building was about 300 feet wide and 400 feet deep.

The second floor plan was labeled *Typical Rooming House Floor*. At a glance, one could see that each rooming floor contained 20 rooming units.

The third floor plan was labeled *Typical Rooming Unit*. This plan showed that as a tenant entered the vestibule of his rooming unit, he passed a parlor on his left and a drawing room on his right. If he walked straight ahead, he soon crossed side halls on his right and left, each of which led to two guest rooms. Each of the guest rooms was about half the size of the standard rooms, which came next. Proceeding down the main central hallway, you encountered 16 numbered rooms, odd numbers on the left and even numbers on the right. The floor plan indicated that each of these rooms was about 12 feet wide 18 feet deep. At the far end of the central hallway were two rooms, each twice the size of a standard room. The room on the left was the kitchen, while the one on the right was the dining room. Across the entire back of the rooming unit, stretching about 40 feet wide and with a depth of 20 feet, was an outdoor balcony.

The final floor plan was labeled *Penthouse Solarium*. There seemed to be about half a dozen swimming pools, a dozen spas, an extensive lounge area, numerous bars and so on. A great place to relax after a day spent working, or a day spent doing nothing much at all.

Hollister did a little mental arithmetic, and concluded that each building, fully occupied, would hold 3200 tenants, with accommodations for an additional 800 temporary guests. Pondering all this, Hollister moved down the central hallway to Room 8 on his right. This room was not locked, so Hollister simply turned the knob and walked in.

The first thing that caught Hollister's eye was a purple and white Northwestern pennant, exactly like the one that had been prominently displayed in the recreation room of his Evanston, Illinois home back on Earth. Scanning the room's contents, the new tenant in Room 8 noted a comfortable-looking double bed, a desk, a large bookcase 3/4 full of books, an easy chair, a reading lamp, an office chair on wheels, a table about 3 by 6 feet, which had some interesting looking equipment on it, and a smaller table on wheels, on whose shelves were some more very intriguing items.

An oil painting on one wall showed a British Brig, Circa 1800, pitted in mortal combat against a ship of similar size flying the Jolly Roger.

Glancing through the titles of the books in his bookcase, Hollister found many old friends he knew he'd enjoy reading again, and a lot of new titles he was sure he was going to enjoy just as much.

After the first perusal, Hollister took another careful look around, and he realized what was missing. There was no closet, no dresser and most surprising of all, no bathroom. Where was a guy to go when he had to pee or take a dump or take a bath or shave or whatever? Then he thought about things a bit more, and realized that ever since he'd been in The Next World, he hadn't felt hunger or thirst or even the slightest need to urinate or evacuate. Things were, indeed, growing curiouser and curiouser!

On his desk, Hollister found a publication entitled "Welcome to Your Next World Rooming Unit."

Seating himself in his very comfortable easy chair, Hollister turned on his reading light, and began to read. "You are spending your first day in your rooming unit. We know you have a lot of questions, and hope this booklet will answer many of them for you. The next few pages are organized on a question and answer basis."

Q. So far everything I have seen and experienced seems too good to be true. What's the catch to all this?
A. There is no catch. The Great Minds, who put all this together, simply want to make your stay in The Next World as pleasant as possible. Many of the things which make life on Earth stressful, painful and sometimes downright miserable have been eliminated. These include crime, politics (some would say those two were the same thing), disease, religion, money, pregnancy, jealousy, envy and suffering.

Q. Who are the Great Minds you mention, and what do they have to gain from running a Utopia like this?
A. You wouldn't recognize their names, as they were never famous when they were alive. Yes, they do get something out of all this—the satisfaction that they have provided everyone here with an after death existence which exceeds anything the most optimistic of humans could ever have dreamed of.

THE NEXT WORLD

Q. Who pays for all this?
A. Don't worry about it. The same great minds that dreamed all this up figured out how to provide it for nothing.

Q. Is all of this real?
A. That's a very astute question. Let's just say that it's as real as it needs to be.

Q. When did all of us in this rooming unit die?
A. In most rooming units, all the residents died on the same day, although they could have been born as much as 90 years or so apart. In those instances when an original resident of a rooming unit leaves that unit, usually to recycle into another lifetime on Earth, a replacement, who may have died almost anytime, will be assigned to that unit.

Q. What is that strange looking equipment I see in my room?
A. Those are truly wondrous items not yet available on the market at the time of your death, but which will become readily available before the end of the 20th Century on Earth. We have made special arrangements to let you have the use of this equipment now. The items on the rolling cart are a color television set, a video cassette recorder and a radio which also plays and records audio cassette tapes and plays compact discs, which are a great advancement over early phonograph records. You had radios on Earth when you lived there, but this one is a tremendous improvement.

   The items on the special table include a computer, a monitor, a keyboard and a computer printer. Manuals and supplies for all of these items are in your desk.

Hundreds of video taped movies, including dozens of silent classics, and virtually every "talkie" produced between the late 1920's and the present date, are available for check-out from the library in your building. Thousands of books are also available for building residents to borrow and enjoy.

Q. What's a computer?
A. In simple terms, a computer is an electronic device which can help you store data, which can let you write a story, a poem, an article or even a book, which can let you test your skill in dozens of games, from the simple to the most complex, and so on. Your computer can be immensely valuable to you, and you will actually use it every day.

    Let's try out a simple demonstration right now. Please go to your computer table, flip the power switch to "ON" and wait a moment. A list of choices called a menu will appear on your screen. Press the letter A, for Attire and then hit the key marked Enter. Insert your All Purpose Card in the special slot in the front of the computer, and hit Enter. This permanently programs the computer in your room to provide perfectly fitting clothing for you. If your guests wish to dress or undress themselves with your computer, using their own cards, this will not disturb your own personal settings.

    From the Attire menu, you may choose daytime wear, evening wear and sleep wear. You'll see that you can choose from an assortment of work clothes, casual wear, and business attire. As with any category, you can also choose to wear nothing. For evening wear, you can choose casual, business attire, formal wear (black or white tie) or, once again, wear nothing. For sleep wear you can choose a nightgown, nightshirt, pajamas or wear nothing.

When no particular pre-set category suits your needs, just type in a description of what you want. If, for instance, you are going to a masquerade party, the system can supply you with a wide range of costumes from which to choose.

When you hit Enter, you will be instantly attired in the manner you have selected. All your garments will be supplied fresh and clean, and they will fit you perfectly. When you are done with the garments, or when you leave the building, the garments will simply disappear. When you return to the building, you will be instantly re-dressed appropriately.

There are spare "attire only" computers located in just about any location in which you find yourself. Should you be in a social, recreational or occupational situation calling for a change in attire, just go to one of these computers, insert your All Purpose Card in the proper slot, and order up any garments you need. Of course, you may always elect to discard what you are wearing and wear nothing, depending on the situation. So, now, try the machine out.

Hollister did so, opting for white tie formal attire. He hit return, and was instantly dressed for a night at the opera, complete with top hat and black patent leather shoes. Having admired himself for a moment in the full length mirror, Hollister hit a few more keys and decided he didn't look that bad wearing nothing but a smile!

Since this was his first opportunity to see himself as he appeared to others in The Next World, Hollister checked himself out. He still stood his familiar 6 foot 3 inches, but his trim muscular body was that of a 30-year old in excellent shape. His handsome face looked as it had when he was 30, and his full head of wavy hair was jet black. Steel grey eyes provided Hollister with perfect vision, and to top everything off, he felt great!

THE NEXT WORLD

Changing once more, this time into a bathrobe, Hollister went back to his reading.

Q. Do I ever eat or drink here, and if I do, what do I do about the evacuation of bodily wastes?
A. In social situations, or any time at all for that matter, you can feel free to eat, drink, even consume liquids which seem in every way to be alcoholic beverages. You will never get drunk, never have a hangover, never gain weight and never have to worry about bodily wastes, which simply do not exist. If you like sweets, or a donut or two with your morning coffee, go ahead and indulge. If your pleasure is cooking and/or consuming wonderful, rich meals, go right ahead. You can have all the fun, and none of the less desirable effects.

Q. What about sex?
A. All you want, whenever you want and with whomever you want. No diseases, no jealousy, no guilt, no pregnancies and you'll find it's the greatest you've ever had!

Q. What kind of a calendar do we use?
A. The same as is presently in use on Earth..

Q. Can I engage in gardening, growing flowers and plants and that sort of thing?
A. Only to a very limited extent. You may dabble with ornamental plantings on your unit's balcony, and perhaps work a bit with the horticulturists who keep things beautiful in the top floor solarium of your building, but that's about all.

Q. Do I have to do any sort of work to earn my keep?
A. Not at all. But, for those for whom life, even life after death, is empty and meaningless without work, there is always volunteer work to be done. Often a person can tailor-make the work he or she does to a particularly strong individual interest. No one is permitted to spend all of his or her time working, however. The one thing we insist on is that our tenants learn to relax and enjoy their non-working hours, too.

Q. So, what all can we do with our free time?
A. You can pursue all manner of interests. Reading, watching movies, listening to music or making it, writing, building various shop projects, pursuing a wide variety of hobby interests, indulging in the fine old art of conversation and much, much more.

Those whose passion in life on Earth was following the exploits of certain athletic teams, whether they were high school, college or professional level, are able to continue following them. Likewise for fans of golf, tennis, and other sports. Those who liked to play golf, bowling, swim, skate, play tennis and so on can still do so. Sadly for winter sports enthusiasts, we couldn't fit in skiing.

We even have catch and release fishing available. Those who like target shooting can indulge in electronic versions that are so realistic that you can almost smell the gunpowder. One group we don't indulge is hunters. The Great Minds don't approve of the killing of wild animals, and that is not part of the scheme of things in The Next World.

Q. What else won't I see here?
A. You won't see automobiles, trains, airplanes, motorcycles or bicycles. Our instant transport system is

ultra efficient, and causes no air pollution whatever. And speaking of clean air, that's the only kind we have. There are no factories fouling the air, and no polluters of any sort fouling our water. There are no tobacco products, so there's no smoking, chewing or snuff dipping.

Q. What about homosexuals?
A. They have their own buildings, and whatever they do within the walls of their own rooming units is entirely up to them.

Q. What if I have other questions, or special needs?
A. Talk with your rooming unit organizer while you have one, or the permanent building advisory personnel later on. These individuals will be happy to help you.

    Hollister set aside the pamphlet he had been reading, asked his computer to supply him with a nightshirt, turned off his computer and went to bed. It had been a long day, and Hollister was ready for a good night's sleep.

Chapter 4

The next morning, dressed in casual clothing, Hollister wandered down to the kitchen. There, while enjoying a breakfast of coffee, grapefruit juice and a superb pecan sticky bun, Hollister met some of his fellow residents of Unit 414 for the first time. The three introduced themselves as Barney Rickley, Room 6, Alma Norton, Room 11, and Henry Petz, Room 14.

"So, here we are," said Rickley, "in what they call The Next World. I have to admit that I never believed there would be any such place. Having given the matter a fair amount of thought from time to time, it seemed to me that death would be the end, a great big nothing, sort of an eternal, dreamless sleep. How about the rest of you?"

"I really didn't know what to expect," Alma Norton offered. "There were periods of my life when I went to church regularly, read the Bible a lot, and got all worked up over whether my life on Earth would qualify me for an afterlife in Heaven. During other stretches, I simply quit worrying about the whole business, and paid very little attention to religion."

"I was an ardent Catholic, myself," Petz added to the conversation. "As a youngster I was an Altar boy, and a bit later on I almost decided to go into a seminary and prepare myself to become a priest. I discovered girls, though, and decided against the priesthood. All my life, nevertheless, I attended church, went to confession regularly, and generally hoped that the reasonably decent life I led on Earth would one day qualify me for a place in the Kingdom of Heaven. All of this is, to put it mildly, an incredible surprise."

Once the other three had offered their comments, they turned toward Hollister expectantly. "Well," Hollister began, "I guess you could say I was an agnostic. I wasn't ready to out and out disbelieve in God and declare myself an atheist, but there were too many things about the various organized religions I looked into that I just couldn't swallow. Finally I decided to wait and see, and what I've seen so far is amazing!"

"I'll second that," Alma interjected. "Now, let's get off the topic of religion and onto something else, namely our life here in Unit 414, and what's next for us. After I got dressed this morning, I played with my computer a bit and found what amounts to a bulletin board. There's a section dealing with news events back on Earth, a section telling about goings on here in The Next World, and a section about what's happening here in our building, our floor and each rooming unit. There will be a special dinner in the dining room of every unit on our floor tonight. We'll all get a chance to meet everybody in Unit 414, and after dinner we'll have a general meeting lasting a couple of hours."

The others all agreed that the evening meeting should be quite enlightening. Then, seemingly by mutual assent, the breakfasters left the table and went their separate ways.

Back in his room, Hollister dug the manuals for his various electronic devices out of his desk, sat in his easy chair and read through the product literature. When he had read the instructions, Hollister tried out his new "toys", working with them until he felt comfortable and familiar with most of them. Obviously, Hollister thought, it would take him a while to feel confident while using some of the computer programs. But then, what the hell, time was one thing folks in TNW had lots of.

A supplementary booklet, supplied by TNW, explained that regular television broadcasts wouldn't begin for a number of years. Furthermore, most of the movies currently available for viewing via video tapes were in black and white, but more movies in color would be available as the years went by.

Finally, the supplementary booklet went on to explain that TNW had adopted a firm policy of not disseminating any films, books, music or news broadcasts before their actual release dates on Earth. One of the main activities of TNW residents was following day-to-day news. Every individual who cared to do so could arrange to have radio broadcasts from his old hometown, and other stations of his choice, fed to his radio set. Furthermore, he could have pages from his favorite Earth newspaper transmitted to him daily, so he could read them from his television screen. TNW was not going to spoil things for news, sports or comic strip addicts by letting them know what was going to happen in the future.

Hollister was particularly impressed with the quality of the compact disk recordings. He knew they would provide great background music for the many hours he expected to spend reading selections from the endless supply of available books.

Sooner or later, Hollister knew, he would find a productive way to spend some of his time, either working at a volunteer job, or engaging himself in some other worthwhile project. For a while, though, Hollister would content himself with getting to know his unit mates, becoming acquainted with the various facilities his building had to offer, and learning a wealth of other things about the wondrous place in which he now resided. After napping about a half-hour, Hollister selected an adventure novel, began reading, and remained engrossed until it was almost dinner time. Not knowing how much people got dressed up for dinner, Hollister opted for a dark business suit, and all the appropriate accessories. Making his way to the dining room, Hollister beheld all his unit mates gathered together for the first time. They seemed pretty dressed-up, so he figured he had guessed right on attire.

Chapter 5

Before, during and immediately after a delicious roast turkey dinner with all the trimmings, Hollister became acquainted to a limited degree with all his fellow tenants of Unit 414. When everyone had finished eating, and the tables had been cleared, Sandra Richards informally called the unit meeting to order.

"All right, everybody, let's settle back and learn something about each other. You were each given name tags to wear whenever they seem appropriate when we are together here in the rooming unit. Soon we'll all know each other well, and the tags will no longer be necessary.

"Just as people travelling on an ocean liner often find that the fellow passengers they get to know best are the ones at their assigned dinning room table, the people you will know best, and who will soon be like a family to you, are your fellow unit mates here in Rooming Unit 414. By the way, the computers in each of your rooms now have a menu listing for Unit Mates which you can refer to.

"Right now, I'd like you each to stand and introduce i yourselves, in room number order, and tell us all something about yourself, and your just finished life on Earth. All of you members of Unit 414 already have one thing in common, you died on Friday, October 6, 1933. Just as most of you no doubt remember playing the game 'You Show Me Yours and I'll Show You Mine' when you were children, it's only fair that I tell you my story, too. As a matter of fact, I'll start things off.

"I'm Sandra Richards, I currently occupy Guest Room

A, and I was 47 years old when I died in a train wreck on August 17, 1901. I was a school teacher in Boston. I never married, and I led what by some standards could be considered a dull life. Although in my earlier years I assumed that one day the great love of my life would come along, sweep me off my feet, marry me and join me in living happily ever after, it just never happened.

"Once I had concluded that it was downright foolish to keep saving myself for marriage, I did engage in a few affairs, and even some one night flings. It's ironic that just about a month before I died, I met a man named Charles Johnston, and things seemed about to change. We rapidly became very fond of each other, and Charlie and I were actually on our way to enjoy a one week honeymoon, without benefit of clergy, when our train derailed and I was killed. Charlie survived, partially crippled as I have since learned, and I ended up here in The Next World. Charlie finally passed on in 1915, and he and I do see each other every now and then.

"The Great Minds, who established this place, opened TNW for business as of January 1, 1900. To them it seemed appropriate to begin the new century with a new form of afterlife for the souls of the departed. Before that time, as I understand it, things were pretty much hit or miss. Some souls were immediately reincarnated, or recycled as we now say, some were put into what you could call cold dead storage, and some simply slipped through the cracks and became the proverbial 'lost souls.' By and large the afterlife situation was a real mess. I've been eternally grateful that I died when I did.

"Coming in near the beginning, I found opportunities to be helpful almost at once. As you have discovered by now, there are no children here in TNW. There are, however, many who were infants or children when they died. We of the teaching persuasion were called upon to help the Great Minds develop a means of enhancing the minds of the souls of those who had died young. That way those souls would have adult-type minds in their adult-type bodies. It was a tremendous challenge to us, and I like to feel we met it remarkably well.

"Anyhow, over the years I've worked at a number of volunteer assignments here in TNW, and for the last eight years or so I've been doing what I am now, helping groups of new arrivals mold themselves into cohesive units, which function efficiently and give all members a sense of belonging. Now, I think I've talked long enough, and it's time that each of you has the floor for a while. Eleanor, let's hear from you."

A striking looking redhead of medium height, and appearing to be about 25 years old, rose to address the group. "I'm Eleanor Atkinson, Room 1, and I was 17 when I died. My boyfriend and I, and another couple, were heading home from a party after a high school football game. One of the kids had raided his father's supply of bootleg hooch, and I'm afraid we all had too much to drink. Bill was driving too fast. He missed a curve, went off the road and smashed into a huge tree. I died instantly, and my guess is that all of the others did, too. I hope I'll have a chance to check up on the others, and perhaps get to visit with them, too.

"Since I was pretty young when I died, I hadn't had anything you could call a career. I was a cheer leader, I liked music, and at 17 you can be sure I liked boys. On those rare occasions when I wondered what I might like to do for a living, I thought about nursing, being a secretary or even being a cook. I imagine I really figured I'd get married, raise kids and let my rich husband support me.

"It's kind of neat being able to see what I would have

looked like at about 25. I know I have a lot to learn, and I hope there's something I can find to do to make myself useful, too. Oh, by the way, I lived in Bettendorf, Iowa." Eleanor took her seat again, and a man who looked to be almost 40 stood up.

"I'm Cedrick Grimes, Room 2, and I was 39 when I died. When I was last healthy and alive, I looked just about the way I do now. I lived in Detroit, where I worked on the production line at The Reo Motor Car Company. After graduating from high school in 1912, I worked in a garage and got what you might call on the job training at fixing cars.

"During the Great War I was in the Army, mainly as a driver in the Transportation Corps. I got to France toward the end of the war, and one day I got too close to an exploding German mustard gas shell. After six months in various military hospitals, I received a medical discharge.

"When I felt able to look for work, I applied at Reo. With my mechanical background, Reo was happy to hire me. That was in 1919, and until I came down with Tuberculosis in late 1932, I built cars. After I got sick I spent the rest of my days in a TB sanitarium, where I died. I left behind a wife, two half-grown children, and not an awful lot more. I hope they get along all right, but there's not much I can do about it now.

"Other than hoisting a few with the boys after work, and going to a Tigers game once in a while, I really didn't do much. The most exciting family vacation we had was one summer when we rented a cabin on a lake and got out fishing a few times." Grimes sat down rather abruptly, and after a few moments a pleasant but rather plain-looking woman, who looked about 30, arose.

"I'm Anne Royston, Room 3, and no, when I was alive

I was not a nun. In fact, my line of work couldn't have been much further removed from life in a religious order, except—," Anne hesitated, then continued. "To tell the truth, I started out at 18 working as a prostitute in Fresno, California. I wasn't very good looking, but with careful costuming and use of cosmetics I got by in the looks department, and I loved my work! Luckily, I managed to stay away from booze, drugs, pimps and other hazards that could have loused me up.

"The lady who ran the place, let's face it, she was the madam, treated all her girls fairly and decently. Sally, that was her name, took a 30% cut and paid the rest of our earnings over to us. If we asked her to, Sally would put a share of our earnings into various investments on our behalf. Since I had few expensive habits, my savings and investments grew. Things were going fine, and I was negotiating with Sally with an eye toward buying her out and taking over the business. At that time Sally was about to be married, and she planned to retire from whoring.

"Then, on a date familiar to you all, October 6, 1933, everything went to hell. It was early evening, just about dinner time, and I was entertaining Harry Klaus, one of my regulars. Harry had stopped by for a quickie on his way home. We had just really gotten going when Harry's wife, I recognized her from a picture Harry had shown me once, burst into the room, pulled a revolver from her coat pocket, and emptied the damn thing into the two of us. She was a good shot, too, and Harry and I were both dead, dead, dead.

"So, here I am. In life my work was screwing, and sex was my hobby, too. If any of you need some pointers or a little action, please let me know. Here, as I understand it, we don't have to worry about jealous spouses or outraged lovers, and nobody has to pay, either."

Anne sat down, and a man whose bearing clearly marked him as a gentleman, stood up.

"Thank you, Anne, your candor was truly refreshing. I'm Bryce Wilkinson, Room 4, and I died at the age of 50, while, believe it or not, I was dining in a fine New York restaurant. There I was, seated at the best table in the place, and enjoying prime fillet mignon. My wife Alice and I were celebrating our 27th wedding anniversary and, I fear, talking while we were eating. Somehow I choked on a piece of steak, which became lodged in my windpipe and cut off my air. As various members of the restaurant staff, and other diners, gathered around and tried to be helpful, I suffocated. I was a Wall Street broker, who had survived the crash of 1929 and emerged richer than ever, worth maybe sixty million dollars, and a quarter's worth of beef did me in!

"My main passions in life were stamp collecting and following college football. I graduated from the University of Wisconsin in 1904, just five years after the immortal Pat O'Dea. During my boyhood I lived in Madison, and I managed to see O'Dea and the Badgers play several times. O'Dea was from Australia, and he soon became nick-named 'The Kangaroo Kicker.' He could punt, drop kick and place kick incredibly well, and he played fullback, too.

"In one game, O'Dea carried the ball 100 yards for a touchdown, and on another occasion he kicked a 60-yard drop kick, while on the dead run, in a game against Minnesota in 1899. One of the greatest days of my young life was the one on which my father arranged for me to meet Pat O'Dea, and persuaded him to autograph a football for me. It was one of the old fashioned footballs, much rounder than the ones they use nowadays, and remained one of my prize possessions all my life.

"You can't believe how pleased I am that I'll be able to follow Badger football and basketball, by radio and in newspaper pages on my television screen. My wife and family are presumably doing fine, and I don't expect to waste a lot of time worrying about them.

"Give me a chance to be useful around here, and I'll be glad to pitch in. Somehow, I'd find it far tougher to sit around and not do much of anything." With that, Wilkinson seated himself, and a vivacious blonde, who looked about 28, stood up.

"I'm Thelma Smithback, Room 5. I was never a hooker, but had I ever needed money badly enough I wouldn't have hesitated to try the world's oldest profession. As it worked out, my parents were able to send me to college. After I graduated from Ohio University with a degree in Journalism, I was fortunate enough to land a job with one of the large national weekly magazines. Due to what could only be described as an extremely fortuitous string of circumstances, I met the publisher, we fell in love, and we got married. My career became one of homemaker and all that entails, as the wife of a prominent and well-to-do man.

"All went well for many years until, at the age of 65, I suffered a fatal stroke. I had a good life and no regrets. Now, with this delightful 28 year old's body and energy to match, I'm ready for whatever comes along. My hobbies in life, by the way, included gardening, reading and collecting antique furniture." Roughly 30 seconds after Thelma had concluded her brief and to the point remarks, Barney Rickley was addressing the group.

"Good evening, fellow inmates of Unit 414. I'm Barney Rickley, Room 6. Never in my lifetime of 72 years did I think I'd someday be appearing before a group like this in a place like this. I mean, talk about dead audiences!" After the ensuing laughter subsided, Rickley continued. "I grew up in St. Louis, and from the time I got an idea of what an entertainer was, I wanted to be one. Somehow, when I told jokes, people laughed. When I gave a serious declamation, people seemed enthralled, and when I was through they applauded, a lot. When I had to think fast, and made up an outlandish excuse to my parents after I had been up to some kind of mischief, somehow my parents believed me—at least most of the time.

"By the time I was in grade school, I was in school plays, operettas and pageants at every opportunity. We put on carnivals during the summer, and I missed no opportunity to attend the show every time a circus, carnival, chautauqua, play, musical, medicine show, traveling evangelist or big time politician came to town. I appeared in just about every production my high school put on, and particularly enjoyed the comedies.

"It went about the same way during my college days, except that I often entertained in saloons and music houses, too, and started making some pretty good money at it. As you might expect, over the years I performed in vaudeville shows, burlesque houses and, yes, on the legitimate stage.

"Many women came and went in my life. I was married six or seven times, and had lots of lady friends, too.

"Inevitably, after I reached a certain age, my career fell into decline and I was more or less forced into retirement. I'd made a pile in my heyday, and had enough left to let me to spend my last years in a retirement home filled with old actors, actresses, comics and other entertainers. We had a ball, and I'm happy to say that when the grim reaper came for me, I was contentedly snoring in a comfortable bed.

"Now, if I can just find a few good writers who can work up some new material for me, maybe it's time for my great comeback!" Rickley bowed to his audience, received a round of applause, and sat down. He was succeeded by Theresa Martin.

"As they say in show business, folks, that's an awfully tough act to follow! I'm Theresa Martin, Room 7, but please call me Terry. I've been part of a Girl Scout troop, a high school glee club, a sewing circle, a charity fund raising group and lots of other organizations over the years, but never did I think I'd belong to a bunch who had all died on the same day!

"I was born and raised in Olathe, Kansas. I married there, raised a family of 4 youngsters there, and died there of a heart attack when I was 67. My husband George ran a dry goods store, and when I wasn't busy with the family I helped out in the store. Somehow we never traveled much at all. Outside of our honeymoon in Omaha, and the time we went to Norman, Oklahoma for our son's graduation from the University of Oklahoma, we never went more than fifty miles from home. Now what's left of me is an awful long way from Olathe, and I don't remember a thing about the trip here!

"I'm ready for whatever comes along, and it's been a real pleasure meeting you all." With that, Terry sat down and it was Hollister's turn.

"Good evening everyone, I'm Art Hollister, Room 8. I have to say it is a great pleasure to be here, compared to the place where some of my Bible-thumping friends back in Evanston always swore I'd end up! I died in a fire at the age of 59, accompanied by my longtime sweetheart, Amy

Lawrence. Amy, the one great love of my life, lived with me for the last 20 years of that life.

"The football and basketball teams whose fortunes I follow closely are those of Northwestern University, of which I'm a proud member of the Class of 1896. I have no interest in professional baseball. I was just beginning to follow the Chicago Bears professional football team when I died. Maybe I'll continue to keep an eye on them, too.

I'm pleased that there's at least one other Big Ten alumnus in our group, even though Bryce Wilkinson *is* a Wisconsin graduate. I'm sure Bryce and I will enjoy following the exploits of the Badgers and the Wildcats in the years to come. Who knows, among the next eight of you there may be an avid fan or grad of one of the other Big Ten schools.

"So, I guess I'm supposed to tell you something of my past, sordid or otherwise. After graduating from college, where my major was a joint one in Mechanical Engineering and Business Administration, I drifted out east and became involved in, of all things, the early days of the motion picture business. I even directed a couple of one reel movies in 1908, before I concluded that the industry's practices were strangling progress.

"At that time I returned to the Chicago Area, and put my mechanical engineering training to work in a firm that made plumbing fittings and fixtures. With a modest inheritance from my father's estate, plus some other funds I was able to raise, I bought the manufacturing plant in 1915.

"Two years later, we were up to our ears in war contracts. We were able to make a contribution to the war effort, and a tidy profit, too. After the Great War, our business expanded and prospered. By the time I died a week ago, our company was grossing about 100 million dollars a year, we had over 500 employees, and things were going extremely well.

"Truth of the matter is, if I put my mind to it, I could probably be running this whole lash-up in a few years. Although you needn't worry about that right away, there is one thing you can be sure of. When I'm ready, I'll find a niche for myself somewhere around TNW, and I'll make a major contribution! Now, Miss Richards, I'd like to make a suggestion. Since none of us has to be anywhere special tomorrow morning, let's continue this meeting at, say, 10:00 a.m."

"That's a fine idea, Mr. Hollister. If there are no objections, we'll meet here at mid-morning tomorrow."

Chapter 6

At the Saturday morning meeting, the first person to stand and address the group was a tall, striking woman with raven tresses. She appeared to be about 28.

"Good morning everyone, I'm Melissa Carpenter, Room 9. I was 85 when I died of old age, as they say. I haven't looked like this for a long, long time. I was born in the Indian Territory in 1852. My mother was a full-blooded Sioux, my father a missionary who worked among several different Indian tribes during his wandering days.

"In 1877, on a visit to Chicago, I met John Carpenter. A former Union Army officer, John had settled in Chicago after the Civil War, and gone into the banking business. John later told me that he had been "smitten" the first time he laid eyes on me, as I sat on a park bench. Working up his nerve, John struck up a conversation with me and, as they say, one thing led to another.

"I extended my visit to Chicago, John and I saw each other frequently, and six weeks after we met in that little park, John and I were married. I never went back to the area of my birth, which became part of Oklahoma when that state entered the Union in 1907.

"John and I had a long and wonderful life together. We raised a family of six children, all of whom went on to successful lives of their own, and all of whom joined John and me when we celebrated our 50th Wedding Anniversary in 1927. We had a lot of our money in the stock market, and suffered severe losses in the 1929 stock market crash. Although we still had plenty to live on, those losses bothered John tremendously, and he began to go downhill quite rapidly, both mentally and physically. Finally, in early 1931, John passed away. As you know, I followed him in death a little over two years later.

"It seems that my whole life was centered around my husband and family. I miss John tremendously, and if he hasn't already recycled I hope to visit him here in TNW." Without mentioning any personal interests, Melissa relinquished the floor to the next speaker, a red headed man who looked a youthful 22.

"Hello, folks, I'm Rod Mitchell, Room 10, and I look exactly as I did 8 days ago, before I made the mistake of picking the wrong Italian restaurant when I went out to dinner. When gunfire broke out, I didn't duck quickly enough, and a stray bullet did me in.

"I didn't care much for school, and at 16 I quit the classroom and went to work as a clerk in a grocery store. I was actually with some friends, celebrating my promotion to assistant manager of the store, on the night I was killed. Gee, come to think of it, that makes at least two of us who died of gunshot wounds.

"I lived in Jersey City, followed the Brooklyn Dodgers, and went over to see them play a few times. Beyond that, I really didn't have a lot of outside interests." With that, young Mitchell sat down and was followed by a pleasant looking lady with short, dishwater blonde hair. This one Hollister had had breakfast with the previous morning, and he looked forward to hearing what she had to say.

"Good morning, everybody. I'm Alma Norton, Room 11. Sorry, Art and Bryce, I'm not that third Big Ten sports fan you're looking for. I'm from Arizona, and I can tell you more than you'll ever want to hear about life on a citrus ranch, irrigation, smudge pots and all that stuff. I grew up on a fruit ranch, went through high school, married the boy next door—that was a mile away as the buzzard flies—and soon we were running our own ranch. The years went by, we did pretty well, and then, the year I was 47, we decided to take a special vacation.

"Our trip took us to coastal Louisiana, and we went there during the fall duck hunting season. We hired a guide, bought the proper licenses and all that sort of thing. The one thing the guide couldn't control was the weather. It was bone chilling, and the rain poured down in buckets. The sniffles I started out with became a heavy chest cold. Before we could even think of heading for home I saw a doctor, who determined that I had a raging case of pneumonia. I was put in the local hospital, I can't even remember the name of the town it was in, and two days later I died.

"During my life I liked to watch birds, and as one of my hobbies I raised peafowl. During the winters I found time to knit, crochet and sew. Sam and I never had any kids, although we both would have liked to. So, my life just ended was rather limited in scope. I'm looking forward to experiencing what TNW has to offer, at least for a good while. After that I may decide to recycle." Alma took her seat again, and was followed by a dark haired man of medium height. He looked about 35.

"Good morning, my friends, I'm Fred Feingold. Until my death at age 58, I lived in Munich, Germany. I was a jeweler with a well-to-do clientele, and life was good until the Nazis came into power. One day some damned Storm Troopers came into my place of business, and began helping themselves to my merchandise. I cursed them and tried to chase them away. For my efforts, they beat me to death right there in my shop. What's to become of my family I have no idea.

"So, on the lighter side, what did I enjoy? I liked classical music, particularly symphonies and similar pieces. I wasn't much of an opera lover. I liked art of all sorts, and spent hours enjoying the displays in various museums and galleries. The creation of special customized pieces of jewelry gave me a great deal of personal satisfaction, too. Maybe I could get interested in American style football, if one of you would be kind enough to explain it to me. In Europe the big sport was soccer.

"I look forward to getting to know all of you much better, and am very pleased that diversity of language is not part of our situation here in TNW. All the different tongues lent a certain flavor to things, but they certainly were a barrier to mutual understanding." On that note Feingold sat down, and was succeeded by an absolute knockout of a long-haired, long-stemmed honey blonde.

"Hi, everyone, I'm Nina Stivers from lucky Room 13." The lady waited a few moments, as if expecting at least the male part of the group to greet her with whistles and applause. When that didn't happen, Nina continued.

"So, you want to know something about me, huh? Okay, here goes. It seems like I was born about age 18 or so, with this delightful face and body. Over a stretch of about 10 years, until I was 28, I did a lot of things, some naughty and some nice. I posed nude for artists and photographers, appeared in several stag films, was a stripper in a burley Q house, was a rich man's mistress until I screwed him to death, and then I put in a stint as a gangster's moll. Unfortunately, it was that last bit that did me in. I got hooked on Heroin I stole from Torpedo John's inventory. One day I accidentally got hold of some uncut stuff, overdosed, and ended up on a marble slab. Oh well, it was a wild life while it lasted!" With that, Nina again took her chair, to be followed by a lanky, slow speaking gent who appeared ageless, but was probably in his late thirties.

"Good morning. I'm Henry Petz, Room 14, and I'm still shaking my head in amazement that a place like this exists. All my life, which ended when I died of diabetes at age 52, I was an ardent Catholic. At one point, in fact, I considered becoming a priest.

"My career consisted of one job, or at least of working for only one employer. I went to work for the telephone company when I was 18, doing all sorts of odd jobs. Sometimes I delivered messages, sometimes I filled in as an operator, for a long stretch I was involved in outside plant construction. That period was followed by several years of inside plant work, then office management and so on.

"Although I had no education beyond high school, I took naturally to the telephone business, and advanced steadily. When I was 50, I was made Vice-President of Operations in the huge general office in Cincinnati. My career was set, so it seemed, but my body refused to cooperate. First my diabetes blinded me when I was 51, then it wiped me out completely less than a year later.

"Between my strict Catholic upbringing, my life full of masses, confessions, prayer and Bible reading, and my steady, nose to the wheel job from an early age, it's a wonder that I ever found somebody to marry me. I did, though, meet a very nice young Catholic girl who worked in the information section at the phone company. Elaine became my wife, we raised a family of four girls and two boys, and we had the satisfaction of seeing them all reach maturity, or some semblance thereof.

"Looking back on it all, I don't really think I had very much fun." Soon after Petz sat down, the last as yet unheard-from woman in the group arose. Though the lady's hair was short and rather nondescript, she was not unpleasant to look at. About 5 foot 6 inches in height, and appearing to be about 30 years old, this gal had a definitely athletic mien.

"Hello there, fellow 414ians. I'm Roberta Jones, Room 15. Yes, people call me Bobbie, and yes, golf is, or was, an important part of my life. With a name like I have, how could I stay away from the links? I grew up in southeastern Texas, and was able to play golf most of the year. In due time I became a professional golfer, playing in ladies' tournaments around the country and earning a pretty good living at it.

"Then, 8 days ago, I was playing a particularly rocky and hilly course in California. Searching for a lost ball, which I was sure had stopped well short of a cliff, I stepped on a chunk of rock that had obviously been a disaster waiting to happen. The rock crashed 150 feet into the canyon below, and I went with it. That sort of thing can really ruin a round of golf!

"I was 32 when I died, and probably had a few more good years on the tour ahead of me. I never had much time for men, even though I had nothing against them. A couple of times I stood up for friends who got married, but I died as single as I was on the day I was born.

"My life was pretty one dimensional, and I expect to broaden my outlook a bit during my time here in The Next World. I've heard there are a lot of golf courses around here, though, so who knows how things will work out?"

After Roberta sat down, the last of the unit mates stood up. This guy stood about 6' 4", looked like he weighed about 265 pounds, and definitely seemed the type who devours half-backs as a mid-afternoon snack. Looking everyone over a bit, as if to intimidate the opposition, the behemoth finally began to talk.

"I'm Clayton Farnsworth, Room 16. Okay guys, you have your third Big Ten football fan. In fact, not to be modest about it, there was a three-year stretch when yours truly pretty much personified Big Ten football. As a fullback I was almost unstoppable, my blocking was devastating and my defensive play as a linebacker was awesome. After college, I had six pretty good years in professional football, too.

"Unfortunately, my luck ran out in practice last week. We were working on scoring in short yardage situations. The center passed the ball directly back to me, and the line opened up a big hole that I went roaring through. Then pow, Joe Makowski, my old buddy Joe, got into the spirit of things and hit me harder than I've ever been hit before. I went cartwheeling through the air, hit the ground hard, broke my neck and died instantly.

"So now, fellows, I suppose you're wondering which Big Ten team I'll be cheering for. Tell you what, I'll sing a few bars and give you a clue."

In a surprisingly fine baritone, Farnsworth began to sing. He'd only sung five words when Hollister and Wilkinson turned to each other and said, in unison, "Oh, shit. A Michigan man!"

Chapter 7

On that Saturday, October 14, 1933, a close friendship began that was to last as long as both Art Hollister and Bryce Wilkinson inhabited The Next World. It wasn't because both had been wealthy men in their previous lifetimes, or really for any tangible reason. There was no denying that their avid interest in Big Ten football and basketball was a strong factor in building their comradeship, even though they cheered for different teams, but there was a lot more to it than that. Both men had acute and inquisitive minds, a great deal of common sense, and the ability to persuade and lead people. They instinctively realized that had they known each other back on Earth, and pooled their resources, they could have created a vast business empire.

Where their new friendship might lead wasn't really on their minds that afternoon, though, as they alternately tuned in to the radio accounts of the Northwestern vs Stanford game from Soldier Field (it ended in a dreary 0-0 tie) and the Wisconsin vs Illinois game from Champaign (that one resulted in a 21-0 shutout of the Badgers by the Fighting Illini).

Luckily, the beer they were drinking was cold and delicious, while the pretzels they munched were crisp, salty and very tasty. No matter how much they consumed, they never had to make pit stops. Art and Bryce agreed that that was probably the greatest thing of all about TNW. Of course, they hadn't sampled the sex yet, and that might be fantastic, too!

Wilkinson switched off the radio and turned to Hollister. "You know, Art, we're in an incredible situation. On Earth, I used to define life as a series of problems and their solutions or attempted solutions. Here in TNW, real problems are, shall we say, in short supply. All of the human misery, the sort of stuff that used to keep lawyers, cops, judges, doctors, undertakers, politicians, ministers and a lot of others busy, has been eliminated."

"Yeah, Bryce, I know what you mean. Right now our biggest problem is back on Earth, one we can't do a thing about. I'm speaking, of course, about the fact that both Wisconsin and Northwestern seem to have lousy football teams this year."

"You've got that right, Art, and they don't even play each other this year. I was, though, really talking a little more seriously. Here in TNW, we don't have to worry about accidents or illness, since everyone is already dead. We don't have to worry about taxes, whether we'll be able to meet the next payroll, where our next meals are coming from, how we can keep a roof over our heads, whether some idiot, or bunch of idiots, will plunge the world into war, whether our kids will get into trouble, and on and on and on."

"Right again, Bryce. It seems that the most valuable assets we have left over from our last lives are our minds. We still have the ability to observe, analyze, and develop opinions. Whatever communication skills we used to have, we still have. How much we'll be able to influence things around us remains to be seen, but obviously there are some things we can accomplish. You remember how I suggested that our unit meeting last night be continued this morning, and how Sandra Richards went along with the idea without any argument. That shows us that, at least within limited areas, residents are able to contribute ideas and suggestions which may be acted upon."

"You've hit on something there, Art, and that's what I see as the kind of thing that will keep people like you and me occupied here. We're the breed who need challenges, some big and some small. Something to keep the juices flowing, so to speak. Now, I've got an idea. Suppose we call up a couple of the ladies from here in the unit, and see if they'd care to join us in the parlor for some get-acquainted conversation. Who would you be particularly interested in getting to know, if you get my drift?"

"That, my friend, is a terrific idea. I'm sure we'll get next to all the women in our unit sooner or later, but to start with, I'd like to get to know Alma Norton."

"Fair enough," Wilkinson rejoined. I think my first choice is Thelma Smithback"

Each man telephoned the lady of his choice, and both found the ones they called very receptive to the idea. Half an hour later, the four were comfortably seated on a couple of facing love seats in the parlor.

"Goodness," commented Thelma Smithback, "it sure is pleasant to get out and visit with someone. They really have this room nicely furnished, too."

"That's true," agreed Alma Norton. "It looks like they set this room up with small group conversation in mind. Now, I seem to recall that one of Webster's definitions of conversation is 'sexual intercourse.' Do you guys want to get laid right away, or do you really want to talk for a while, first?"

Hollister had, for years, considered himself unshockable, but Alma's honest and direct question took him aback. "Well, yes, Alma, I guess we all figure that we'll be pairing off and heading for bed a bit later on, but I don't see any harm in actually talking to each other for a while before we do. What do you think, Bryce?"

"I agree with you, Art. We have this wonderful situation in which we all know how the evening will end up, and we all look forward to it. For some of us it's been a long time since we could perform the way we know we'll be able to tonight. Let's visit for a while, first, and get to know each other in the non-Biblical sense."

"You win," Alma conceded, "now, what would you like to talk about?"

"Since someone has to start out," Thelma interjected, I'll give it a try. How do all of you like it here in TNW so far? Is it anything like you expected an afterlife would be? I'll answer those questions, too, but I'd like to hear what each of you thinks."

"Okay, Thelma, that gives us something to chew on for a while," Hollister said. "Alma has heard me say this before. During my life on Earth I was pretty much an agnostic with a wait and see attitude. Looks like I guessed right, because in the short time I've been here in TNW I've seen an awful lot. I think the Great Minds, who created this place, did a fantastic job. By eliminating so many causes of stress and strain, they did create a sort of heavenly paradise at that.

"Just think about it. There's no religion, no illness, no jealousy, no envy, no greed, no crime, no money and so on. All of us remember what those things were, however, and we can think and talk about them if we wish. The Great Minds left us with our own minds intact, not full of holes like Swiss cheese. Each of us can take his own approach to life here. We can opt to relax and enjoy it, or seek ways by which it can be improved. We can look for challenges, or go with the flow. We can work, or we can loaf."

"I'm as happy here as a soul could be," Alma chimed in. "During the religious stretches of my life on Earth, I often got myself all worked up, and sometimes actually worried, about the concepts of heaven and hell. When I viewed things more rationally, I figured out that those promulgating various religions were all just guessing. Some promised everyone a glorious afterlife, while others offered the solace of heaven only to those who followed the strict patterns their particular sect prescribed. In many cases, you got the idea that only those who contributed lots of money to a particular religious or quasi-religious group were warranted to have a chance at a happy life in the hereafter. Hell fire and damnation helped make very comfortable livings for a lot of preachers."

"Guess it's my turn," said Wilkinson. "I'm very pleased with the physical set-up here. Who could have expected that each of us would have a private room, a telephone, a radio, a television set, a video tape recorder and even a computer. Some of those electronic items won't, as I understand it, be seen on Earth for years.

"There are a few things I question about the general philosophy of this place, and a lot I don't yet understand. Since we all have as long as we'll ever need to discover everything TNW has to offer, and in many cases to find out what we can offer TNW, there's no pressure, no urgency, no strain.

"I never believed in life after death at all, never went to church. I'm surprised and pleased that TNW exists, and will be even happier when I find something constructive to do here. Okay, Thelma, let's hear from you"

"Fair enough, Bryce. As a trained journalist, I often pondered the question of life after death. Was it real, was it figment of someone's imagination, or was it an out and out sham, mainly a device to keep the collection coffers filled, and the clergy living comfortably? I reasoned that if there was a hereafter I'd eventually find out about it, and if there wasn't, it really didn't matter at all.

"I was exposed to Christian teaching from time to time, but somehow it just didn't ring true. Christians tried to sell the idea that man was created in God's image, but to me it seemed more likely to be the other way around. I couldn't understand how an all powerful God could allow so much human suffering. Most unpalatable of all, I couldn't stomach how so much of man's inhumanity to man over the years had been perpetrated in the name of religion.

"In my book, the finest single thing that the Great Minds did here was to eliminate religion. I'd rank establishing a common language next. The common skin color idea has some merit, but it probably works best when souls are out in public. I want to investigate that matter a bit more, along with a number of other things, some rather deep and some frivolous."

"Let's lighten this up a bit," said Art, "and talk about some of the more trivial things. I'd like to know where our 'food' comes from, what it really is, and how our bodies digest it. I'd also like to know who cooks the food, who serves it and who cleans up afterwards."

"I've been wondering," said Thelma, "whether we can ever take a bath or a shower just for the fun of it, even though we supposedly remain squeaky clean all the time. I'd also like to know about organized social life around here, and what it consists of."

"One thing I want to know," said Bryce," is how we can get in touch with others who have died in the 1900's, with whom we'd like to communicate and possibly visit. If we can visit those fellow souls, how do we go about arranging it?"

"I was checking the bulletin board on my computer just before Art called me," said Alma. "There's a meeting scheduled for Wednesday afternoon at 1:00, in the dining room. Several of the TNW staff will be there for a general question and answer session. All tenants are urged to have questions ready. And now, the main thing on my mind is, will the sex here be as good as it's cracked-up to be? Let's go to bed and find out!"

They did, and it was!

Chapter 8

At the Wednesday afternoon gathering, Sandra Richards once again chaired the meeting. Sandra sat at a rectangular table on the rostrum, accompanied by two people the group had never seen before.

"And now, my friends," Sandra announced, "I'd like to introduce two very special guests. Maria Cortez is Main Administrator of Building KK 280. She and her staff have an office on the first floor, just off the lobby. You can always reach someone there, 24 hours a day, for special information, general advice or help. During this meeting you'll learn about a number of ways the building office can help you. Once every business day, the Main Administrator attends a meeting like this, each time in a different rooming unit in the building. We'll see Maria again in about 40 weeks.

"Our second guest is Stanley Caldwell, Special Liaison Officer to the Great Minds Office. Stanley and his colleagues make only one official visit to each rooming unit, and for us this is it. As long as Stanley remains in his present position, he will always be available for consultation. Stanley is our official conduit to the Great Minds Office—he serves Building KK 280, and 19 others. Should a new person assume the job now held by Stanley, all affected tenants will be promptly advised as to the identity of the new liaison officer."

After official greetings, welcoming remarks and so on by Cortez and Caldwell, the meeting was thrown open for questions and comments by the tenants. Tenants were invited to address any of the three on the rostrum, or to simply ask questions and wait to see who replied.

"I'd like to ask Mr. Caldwell to tell us the kind of things people contact him about," said Roberta Jones.

"I could probably talk for an hour or so on that," Caldwell replied, but I'll resist the temptation. In general terms, I'm an ombudsman for you and about 64,000 other souls here in TNW. When any of you has a problem, a complaint about how things operate here in TNW, a suggestion about how something affecting all of us might be altered or improved, or wants to become involved in some project or position here in TNW which is beyond the scope of your local administrator, I'm the one to come to. You can call my office, and set up an appointment to discuss the matter. Such appointments usually require no more than a week's lead time to set up."

"How," inquired Melissa Carpenter, "should we address women here in TNW, particularly those we don't know personally?"

"Everyone here in The Next World is considered to be single," Sandra Richards replied. "In a business or formal situation, it is appropriate to address a woman as Miss so and so, if you know her last name, or ma'am if you don't. You'll know instinctively when to begin calling a person by his or her first name."

"When we are outside, as naked souls, and want to carry our All Purpose Cards in a safe and convenient manner, how do we do that?" asked Cedrick Grimes.

"I've been meaning to tell you about that," Sandra replied. "Now, watch carefully." Sandra showed the group the underside of her left forearm, to which an All Purpose Card appeared to be stuck fast. "When you try it, you'll find that your card will stick to this part of your arm. The card will stay there until you yourself remove it, and will stick to you regardless of whether you are wet or dry, dressed, undressed or in naked soul status. This makes it easy to carry your card, and almost impossible to lose it."

Next, Fred Feingold asked, "What if I want to look up an old friend or a relative. Can I telephone that person, and can I visit that person or have him or her come to visit me?"

"I'll answer that one," replied Maria Cortez. "It may be easy, or virtually impossible, to do what you describe. First of all, the person you are looking for must be dead. Second, the individual must have died on or after January 1, 1900. Third, you must be able to positively identify the person you seek. Fourth, you must be able to spell the individual's name perfectly. The more obscure and unusual the person's name, the more likely it is you will be able to find him.

"To give this process a try, go to your room, turn on your computer, and select 'Locator' from the menu. You will then be asked to answer a number of questions. The first 11 are:

1. Full Name of person you wish to locate, otherwise enter as much of the name as you can.
2. Date of Birth if known, otherwise leave blank.
3. Date of Death if known, otherwise leave blank.
4. Do you positively know if this person is dead?
5. Person's last known occupation.
6. Person's home address at time of death.
7. Person's place of birth, if known.
8. Person's sex.
9. Where person died, if known.
10. Cause of person's death, if known.
11. Your relationship to person, i.e. parent, spouse, sibling, friend, lover, aunt, uncle, cousin,etc..

"Sometimes the program will prompt you with more questions. If you can answer the questions exactly, you have a very strong chance of finding the one you seek. The more obscure and incomplete your answers, the poorer are your chances of success.

"If you are looking for a 'Bill Smith,' who you think died somewhere in North America during the late 1920's, your chances of success are dismal.

"A few words of caution regarding a search of this type. Please do not enter upon something like this frivolously, which could tie up the search facilities and deny someone else ready access to the program. Hopefully the computer communication capacity here in TNW will be expanded substantially as the years go by. Sometimes, to complete an identification, you may have to choose between a number of photographs shown on your computer screen.

"At any rate, let's assume your searching efforts have been successful. Your screen will show all pertinent information on your individual. This will include your person's building number, floor number, unit number, room number and telephone number. You may telephone the person from your own room, talk with him or her, or leave a message if the individual is not in when you call.

"If both the party you locate and you want to do so, you can arrange a meeting with the person, go out to lunch or dinner or whatever you wish.

If you care to, you can visit someone for up to a week's time every six months or so. Arrangements of this sort may be made through your building office. The individual may visit you, or you may visit him or her.

"The searching process may disclose that a soul you are trying to locate has opted to recycle into a new body on Earth. If so, you are simply out of luck, except that you will have a general idea of what became of the individual."

"I wonder," asked Hollister, "if one of you could give us an overview on the food and drink we consume here. It's delicious, but what is it, really? Why don't we excrete bodily wastes? Where does the food come from, who prepares and serves it, who cleans up afterwards? How do we obtain the necessary foodstuffs when we have the urge to do some of our own cooking? Finally, can we ever go out to eat in a restaurant?"

"That, sir," replied Stanley Caldwell, "touches upon one of the most fascinating facets of The Next World. When the Great Minds created this place, they could easily have left food and drink out of the scheme of things. After all, how much sustenance does a dead person require?

"On the other hand, consumption of food and drink is ingrained in the social lives and customs of people the world over. To remove food and drink from an afterlife, and still make that afterlife a really pleasant one, was nigh onto impossible.

"So, the Great Minds came up with 'Pseudofood.' This nifty stuff gives everyone all the sensations of eating and drinking, and absolutely none of the problems. You never have to go to the john, and you never even pass gas!

"Food preparation and service are handled by volunteers who would rather do that than just about anything. Clean-up is easy, since all traces of this magical food disappear within two hours after the food is prepared.

"When you want to do your own cooking, just call the foodstuffs specialist in your building office, and order whatever you need. Everything will be delivered to your pantry over night, and it all stays in perfect condition until the seals on its packaging are broken. This system does behoove folks to get along with food preparation and consumption, though. Every now and then we hear about someone or, more likely, some group having a party. They dawdle over their food, only to have it disappear before their eyes!

"There are also many fine restaurants here in The Next World. Just check your computerized directory, choose the place you wish to visit, and telephone for reservations. You get great food, there's no bill and no tipping. Chances are that all residents of your rooming unit will often enjoy dining out together. Of course, should you wish, you can go out alone or with special friends. Any approach you choose will be fine."

"That was a good rundown on food, Mr. Caldwell," Bryce Williamson broke in. "Now, how about a similar commentary on racial differences, and how they are handled here?"

"In some respects that has been a lot easier than the food matter, and in others it has been more difficult and complicated. We serve souls of all possible racial backgrounds here, the blackest Negroes from Africa to the palest Scandinavian Nordics. Avoiding potential problems out in public is relatively easy. As you know, when you're outside as a naked soul, everyone is a beige color, facial characteristics are just a bit blurred, and no one knows or cares what color body any soul last inhabited on Earth.

"But, when it comes to screening everyone for assignment to rooming units, problems arise. I am, however, getting a little ahead of my story. For reasons we've not been able to determine, a relatively high percentage of souls which have previously inhabited the bodies of orientals opts for immediate recycling, almost always into babies being born into the same ethnic group those souls belonged to in their previous lives. A lower but still substantial percentage of souls which previously dwelt in the bodies of brown and black skinned people makes a similar choice.

"Now back to the matter of selection and screening. Most of the ex-black and brown souls ask for assignment in rooming units consisting entirely of similar individuals. A slightly higher than average percentage of the ex-oriental souls request placement in units of their 'own kind.'

"The remaining souls ask for housing which reflects, in miniature, the diversity of the Earth's population. In every case, the segregation or lack of it in assigned housing is a direct result of the expressed desires of the tenants. Inside their buildings, which are fully equal in quality and furnishings to those occupied by everyone else in TNW, the skin colors and appearances of the tenants reflect exactly how those people appeared during the prime of their lives on Earth, or how they would have appeared had they lived to maturity.

"The various building populations live and eat as they wish, with one exception. Even though the food is Pseudofood, we don't feed former cannibals on simulated human flesh.

"The few foolish souls who opt neither for recycling nor for the incredible life we have set up for them here, the ones whose only pleasure seems to be in giving others a bad time, are simply, permanently and painlessly eliminated.

"The population assortment of every rooming unit is put together on the same basis. The people selected are deemed by the Wonderful Central Processor to have an extremely high likelihood of getting along very well together, and of becoming to all intents and purposes a happy family."

Bryce Wilkinson was tempted to stand again, and make a snide remark to the effect that, yeah, it was a family, without any problem children. On second thought, however, Wilkinson held his tongue. After all, who the hell needed problem children?

Next, Thelma Smithback arose, to ask questions which seemed rather trivial compared with some which had already been discussed. "I'd like to hear about the organized social life around here, and I'd also like to know whether there's a way to take a bath or shower here, just for the pleasure of it. It's nice being super clean all the time, but still—"

"That's one for me," said Maria Cortez. "As a new building, with a population which is still getting used to TNW, we haven't really gotten into the swing of organized social life.

"So, let's look into the future a bit. Here in your own unit, you have space enough to entertain, for instance, the people from one other unit. It would be a bit crowded, but with the parlor, drawing room and dining room available, plus the balcony when it's warm enough, you have space here for informal parties of moderate size.

"For parties which involve your entire floor, you can reserve one of the party rooms downstairs. The whole top floor can be used for parties, too. Twice a week we'll have a Happy Hour gathering up on the top floor, with hot tubbing, swimming, cocktails, hors d'oeuvres and all the rest. On the average, from what other buildings experience, we can expect about a third of our tenants to show up for any given Happy Hour. Once a year, on New Year's Eve, we'll have a really big party on the top floor. Orchestra, dancing, dinner, the works. On that night we

THE NEXT WORLD 57

may have a turn-out of close to 3,000. It'll be wall-to-wall souls!

"On the top floor, which is open daily for general recreation and relaxation, we have pools, spas, and showers. For those who crave soaking in water, the opportunity is available on the 12th floor."

"What can you tell us about the golf courses here?" asked Clayton Farnsworth.

"Since I've been here a dozen years now, and have had a chance to play a lot of golf, I'll tell you about the situation," replied Stanley Caldwell. "There are thousands of golf courses here, ranging in difficulty from short little par 3, 9-hole pitch and putt courses to good, solid, long 36- hole layouts of championship quality. Somehow, there are always tee times and caddies available.

"The golf courses are our only outdoor recreational facilities, and we all play as naked souls. Everyone who formerly played golf on earth starts out here with playing ability equal to the best he or she ever developed on Earth. Literally hundreds of pros are available to provide lessons. At the pro shop, on your first visit to one of our courses, you will be fitted with a brand new set of clubs. The code for those clubs will be encoded on your All Purpose Card. Every time you head for the links, your clubs will be ready and waiting for you at whatever course you have chosen to play.

"Every five years, you can obtain a new set of clubs. So, when club design improvements come along, you can take advantage of them. In every pro shop there is a wide and wild assortment of golf hats available, in every style and color you can imagine. These hats are the only attire golfers wear, and they help you tell one naked soul from another at up to a hundred yards! Leave your hat with your clubs, and it will follow you around from course to course, too. You can have as many new hats as you wish.

"Full information on all golf courses is available on your computer bulletin board, as is information on all other recreational facilities. All recreational facilities except golf, even our catch and release fishing ponds, are housed inside and available 365 days a year. These facilities include bowling alleys, electronic target and trap shooting ranges, miniature golf and golf driving ranges, tennis courts, pool and billiard halls, ice skating, roller skating and even curling rinks. Whatever your pleasure, we probably have it."

The meeting went on for another half hour, with questions covering all manner of subjects, from the important to the inane. When it was over, the tenants of Unit 414 had a lot to think about. Before beginning his personal pondering, Hollister made his way to the rostrum and extended his hand to Stanley Caldwell.

"Stan, I'm Art Hollister. One of these days, when I've figured out exactly what it will be, I'm going to come to you with a project in mind. All I can promise now is that the project will be noteworthy, of value to the residents of TNW, and perhaps to those of the Planet Earth as well"

"It's a pleasure to meet you, Art," Caldwell replied. "When you're ready, by all means come and see me."

Chapter 9

On Saturday afternoon, this time accompanied by Thelma and Alma, Hollister and Wilkinson were again following football. That day was the high point of Northwestern's season, as the Wildcats defeated the Indiana Hoosiers 25-0 at Soldier Field. That was to be Northwestern's only victory of the season. Wisconsin again fared badly, as the Badgers fell to the Iowa Hawkeyes 26-7 at Iowa City.

After Bryce switched off the radio, and put some good recorded music on to play, Alma had a delightfully indecent idea. "Okay, gang, let's have some fun. First, let's all get naked. Then, Art and I can enjoy a roll in the hay while you two watch. When we're finished, the two of us can watch while you two go at it. After a short break we'll switch partners and start all over again. If you like, and Thelma is willing, the two of us girls can put on a show for you giys, to sort of round things off. You interested?"

Hollister, totally intrigued by the idea, nodded his head. Wilkinson, however, suggested a slight change in the schedule of things.

"Why don't you ladies perform for us first? If that doesn't get Art and me in the mood to party, nothing will!"

Later on, when everyone was sated, Thelma offered a realistic assessment of the situation.

"I suspect that copulation and oral sex are the most popular forms of recreation TNW has to offer. We can take it as a given that as time goes on we'll all screw every member of the opposite sex in our unit, and probably do it with a lot of people from other units, too. Be all that as it may, it will always mean a lot to me, and I hope it will to you, that the four of us were the first to frolic with each other here."

"I couldn't have said it better myself," said Hollister. What do you say that the four of us make it a date to get together on the last Saturday afternoon of every month? That would mean that we'd meet a week from today to start things off."

"I'd say that we've already started things off in great style," Alma commented, "and I'm completely in favor of seeing you three on a regular basis."

The others readily agreed, and thus was born a small and friendly group, destined to meet every month for decades. Between themselves, the members referred to their quartet as the Frolicsome Four.

That night the Frolicsome Four celebrated the formal inauguration of their group by going out to dinner together. They checked the computerized listings for restaurants, found an Italian style place that sounded good, and Wilkinson called and made their reservations. All he had to do was insert his All Purpose Card in a slot in the base of the telephone. The restaurant sent an electronic signal which encoded their reservation for four on the card, and encoded their travel destination as well.

Dressed for dinner, the group proceeded through the lobby of their building, and out onto the sidewalk. When the four naked souls reached the Travel Station outside, each of the group, starting with Wilkinson, inserted his card in the appropriate slot. No sooner had the fourth one, Hollister, retrieved his card than the four of them were whisked away, to arrive only seconds later at a large dining center complex. They easily found their way to Paisano's Palace, where their clothing re-materialized as they entered the building, and they were seated promptly.

THE NEXT WORLD 61

The food was great, and they dug in and enjoyed it. After the main meal, they lingered over servings of spumoni, and chatted for a while.

"I wonder," offered Hollister, "how it is that everyone seems to accept their present situations, and no one complains. Do you think something was done to us all at Central Processing to make us happily accept things here as they are?"

"That's a possibility, Art," said Bryce, "but come to think of it, what do we have to complain about? If there is something we feel needs to be improved or added, there's a mechanism in place which will at least let us make suggestions. How well the process works, and what percentage of suggestions is adopted, is anyone's guess."

"I wish," added Thelma, "that someone had asked Stanley Caldwell the other day whether the Great Minds had any problems, or resounding failures, while they were in the process of setting up TNW."

"I wish," Alma piped up, "that I had some great concern or question to bring up right now. After that great sex this afternoon, and this wonderful meal tonight, I'm ready for a good nap. On second thought, make that about nine hours of shut-eye!"

Chapter 10

The ensuing Wednesday afternoon, October 25, 1933, found the occupants of Unit 414 once again gathered for a unit meeting. This time, Sandra Richards was the only staff member present.

"Time, they say, passes quickly when you're having fun," Sandra began. "In just a couple of weeks I'll be saying good-bye. So, now's a good time for us to hash over what's been going on so far, and perhaps make some plans for the future.

"I know that general TNW policies say no politics, but almost every group has to endure some. With rooming units, for instance, there should be a leader to keep things moving smoothly, and to bring matters of group interest to the attention of the building staff when necessary. Most units handle this on a monthly rotation basis, with the tenant in Room 1 handling the job first, and passing it on to the next person on the first of every month.

"The main thing a Unit Leader should do is to keep a file of every suggestion or complaint brought before the group during his or her tenure. All formal suggestions and complaints should be given to the Leader in writing, dated and signed by the originator. A second person, serving as Scribe, should keep track of the disposition of such matters, and make notes of other things taken up by the group. The scribe job should rotate, too, with the first month's duty falling to, say, the occupant of Room 9.

"All the pertinent records can be entered onto a single high density 3 1/2 inch computer disk, which can be passed on from scribe to scribe for years before a second disk is required.

"Assuming this group adopts that system, I'd suggest that each leader hold at least one unit meeting a month. Just remember that the fewer meetings you hold, the further ahead you'll have to plan something that requires group approval. Now, lets have some input from you"

"I suggest," said Nina Stivers, "that Eleanor Atkinson take over as Unit Leader a week from today, after our last meeting with Sandra, and that Melissa Carpenter assume the post of Scribe on the same day."

A general murmur of assent followed, with no spoken objections, and that matter was settled.

"Now," said Clayton Farnsworth, "let's get on with some serious planning here. A week from yesterday is Halloween, and it's time we organized our first unit party in honor of the occasion. We can have the party by ourselves, or invite the tenants in one of the nearby units, say 413, to join us here. I'll volunteer to organize things, assuming that everyone agrees, and stands ready to help as necessary."

Farnsworth's suggestion was greeted by a round of applause. After a brief discussion, the group voted in favor of inviting their neighbors in Unit 413 to join in the festivities.

"I'd like to know," said Roberta Jones, "what problems the Great Minds had in setting this place up, and whether they had any notable failures in the process."

"I happen to know of some I can share with you," Sandra replied. The Great Minds originally wanted to populate the outdoors here with birds, wild animals of all types, perhaps even some domesticated animals, and pets such as dogs, cats, turtles, rabbits, goldfish and so on. None of this proved practical or even feasible, and those ideas had to be abandoned."

"Can you tell us more," Bryce Wilkinson wanted to know, "about the selection process here in TNW. Which souls get in, and which ones lose out?"

"Having been here almost from the beginning," Sandra answered, I do know a bit more about that than is widely publicized. As you are already pretty well aware, those souls which were the inner beings of horrendous and/or career criminals, who led vicious, violent lives and contributed nothing but grief to their society, are screened out and eliminated.

"The real problem is the borderline cases, the bums, low lifes, near morons, feeble minded and such. On Earth, many of these are the ones who breed like rabbits, and then take no responsibility for their young. They clog the welfare rolls for generations.

"The Great Minds finally settled on the criteria of educability. When they created the Wonderful Central Processor, which has a tremendous capacity, far more than is presently being utilized, they included an ingenious instant education feature. Every mind, in souls being considered for retention in The Next World, is injected with the full equivalent of a fine elementary and secondary school education. The overwhelming majority of those souls proves capable of absorbing and using such an education. Those souls are processed the rest of the way, and offered the choice of immediate recycling, or becoming residents here in TNW. The rest, the absolutely hopeless, are eliminated. One final note on this—the souls whose minds have already received enhancement beyond the high school level are in no way adversely effected by the Wonderful Central Processor's knowledge injection."

"What I'd like to know," said Henry Petz, "is just exactly where is this place?"

"I really can't tell you that, Mr. Petz, mainly because I don't know exactly. What I *can* say is that this place is vast and endless. The capacity to handle souls is in the hundreds of billions. A special form of artificial gravity keeps everything in place. The only facilities not enclosed in buildings are the golf courses. The Great Minds were avid golfers on Earth, and absolutely insisted that there must be golf courses in TNW, and so there are!

"Do you foresee the time when the powers that be here will require certain souls to recycle," inquired Rodney Mitchell.

"I doubt that will happen," Sandra replied. "What I think the Great Minds are assuming is that boredom will set in, and a lot of the soul population here in TNW will ultimately opt for recycling. That would be especially true if conditions on Earth were good, and the souls considering recycling felt assured that the new bodies they would be inhabiting had special potential of one sort or another."

"Does the population here in TNW regard the Great Minds as gods, and worship them," Barney Rickley wanted to know.

"Absolutely not," Sandra declared. "Those who think about it at all are grateful to be here in TNW. The rest are busy enjoying themselves, and don't worry about anything else."

"Do souls here celebrate the various holidays," asked Anne Royston.

"Yes they do, Anne," Sandra replied. "In general, the TNW population tends to observe the major holidays they did while on Earth, but not the minor or religious ones. Thanksgiving is a big one for former Americans and Canadians, and is celebrated more and more by others, when they take the time to consider how much better they have it here than might have been the case.

"We also observe a special day of fellowship and goodwill, which we call simply Midwinter Holiday. This occasion, full of soul-warming good cheer, is looked forward to and celebrated by everyone.

"New Year's day is a very special occasion, too. Former Americans still manage to celebrate the 4th of July, even though the lack of fireworks sort of puts a damper on things. But, a mind is a great thing to use, and ingenuity around here seems to know no bounds!

"Besides the holidays I've mentioned, we all tend to celebrate the birthdays of unit mates. Although in appearance, health and stamina we are all frozen in time, birthdays give us good excuses to have parties."

When Sandra had finished her answer on holidays, the flurry of questions subsided. Sandra left the room, but before anyone else stirred Hollister got to his feet and moved to the podium.

"Friends," Hollister said, "There's another piece of business we need to take care of. Sandra has done an outstanding job of helping us get organized. She will be leaving soon, and it's only right that we give her a proper send-off. I suggest that we make it a really special occasion, a formal farewell dinner, on the evening of Saturday, November 4th. If it's agreeable with all of you, I volunteer to see to all the details. All any of you will have to do is show up for the party, having signed our "Thank You" card before hand. Does anyone have any objections to this idea?"

Encountering absolutely no opposition to the farewell party idea, Hollister went on with a couple of related topics.

"One thing we need around here," Hollister said, "is a social committee. It look's like we'll be having a lot of parties, and someone should be responsible for seeing that things go smoothly when we do. I'll volunteer to serve on the first official Unit 414 Social Committee, and I hope Clayton Farnsworth and Anne Royston will agree to join me, subject, of course, to our group's approval."

Once again the group approved, with the suppressed delight of a bunch who knew they were going to have a lot of fun thanks to the efforts of others.

"Now, there's something else," added Hollister, "that I'd like to check on. Will anyone in the group who sings, plays a musical instrument, or has genuine artistic talent, including the ability to paint, draw, design or letter, please stop and talk with us committee members before you leave? I'd also like to talk with Barney Rickley."

Hollister was pleased to see that six of the group stayed behind, besides Barney Rickley and the three committee members. Drawing Anne and Clayton aside, he thanked them for their willingness to serve on the social committee, then asked Farnsworth to check on musical talent, and Anne to see what kind of artistic ability had come forth.

Beckoning Barney Rickley to him, Hollister suggested that they both be seated. "Barney," Hollister said, "I'd like you to MC the party for Sandra. Having a professional entertainer among our group is our great good fortune, and if you are willing, I foresee calling on you for this sort of thing quite often."

"Art," Rickley replied, "I'd have been crushed if you hadn't asked me. I warn you ahead of time, though, that without my writers to crank out fresh material for me, I may lay an egg now and then. I'll be happy to help out whenever you want me, but I know that others will want to MC some of our parties, too, and that's fine with me."

Thanking Rickley enthusiastically, Hollister promised to get back to him in a few days. Then, turning to see how the others were doing, Hollister noticed that Thelma Smithback was waiting to talk with him.

"Art, you need me on the Social Committee, and I'm here to volunteer. Not only will I bring the man:woman ratio into balance, but I have a great deal of expertise to offer. During my years as the wife of a well-to-do publisher, I entertained a great deal. I had extensive experience dealing with caterers, chefs, decorators, florists, musicians, you name it. I know instinctively whether to decorate and feed lavishly, or whether to tone it down. In short, you can tell me the kind of occasion, give me any special ideas or suggestions you have, and turn me loose. On the day, or evening, of the event, you can be sure that everything will be perfect."

"Thelma," Hollister replied, "I wholeheartedly accept your offer, and welcome you to the Social Committee. Together we'll produce some memorable social events! Now, let's amble over and see what musical and artistic talent we've dredged up here in Unit 414."

The others had left, leaving only Farnsworth and Anne Royston. Hollister told them that Thelma would be joining the three of them on the Social Committee, then asked the trio to be seated. He excused himself, went to the nearby kitchen, and returned with a tray bearing 4 large glasses of iced Super Pseudo Soda. Returning to the table, he distributed drinks to everyone and then took a seat.

"Okay, my friends, what kind of talent did we uncover?"

"Artistically," Anne replied, we had three volunteers. Eleanor Atkinson is an accomplished artist. She was winning prizes in local exhibitions in Iowa when she was 15. I think Eleanor will be fine for producing posters for publicizing our various festivities. Theresa Martin made a lot of signs during her days in the dry goods business, and is an expert at lettering. She also studied calligraphy, and her handwriting is beautiful and amazing. Theresa can help Eleanor with the lettering on posters, and produce invitations and all manner of greeting cards and the like for us. Our most interesting find is Rod Mitchell. He's an accomplished ice sculptor, and if we can find him ice or simulated ice, he says he can create some incredible party decorations for us."

"In the musical area," declared Farnsworth, "we have two. Fred Feingold has concert quality skills as a violinist, but says he can fiddle with the best of them, too. Roberta Jones finally admitted that she had a second passion on Earth, besides golf. From the time she was ten, Bobbie played the tenor saxophone. She was part of her high school and college bands, and continued to study under an excellent teacher, right up to the time she went flying off that cliff!"

"Correction, Clayton, I believe we actually have four musicians. The moment I heard your rendition of *The Victors*, I recognized you as the possessor of a fine, trained singing voice. You were not only a force on the gridiron, but an outstanding singer as well."

"All right, you have me there," replied Farnsworth, "but who's the fourth musician you alluded to?"

"Sooner or later I have to admit a couple of things, Clayton," said Hollister. "I played a little football myself back in the old days, and was Northwestern's starting quarterback in 1895. My uncle, C. M. Hollister, coached Northwestern football for four years, beginning in 1899.

"And, yes, I'm a piano player, too. In college I played a lot of barroom piano, and did the same for a few years afterwards, before I drifted out east and got into the motion picture business. Regardless of what else I was doing for a living, I kept up my interest in playing the piano. Now you know my deepest secrets.

"So, with a piano player, a sax player, a fiddler and a male vocalist, we have the beginnings of a nice little combo. With luck, we can find enough more players here on the floor to put together a respectable musical aggregation. I know someone who might want to work on that project, and I'll keep you informed of progress.

"It looks like we have just the talent we need in the artistic area, too, for posters, invitations and the like. And, by the way, Barney Rickley has graciously agreed to MC our party for Sandra. Now, Clayton, about Halloween......"

Chapter 11

On Saturday, October 28, 1933, the Frolicsome Four had their first official monthly get-together. Since the football season was still in full swing, listening to radio broadcasts of games was important to Hollister and Wilkinson, and politely tolerated by Alma and Thelma. Hollister and Wilkinson adopted a policy under which, when their teams were playing at the same time, they would listen to full alternate quarters, rather than tuning the dial back and forth all the time, which tended to drive the ladies up the walls.

Wilkinson and Hollister also agreed that if, on the days of certain games, one contest was dull as dishwater, and the other was extremely exciting, they would concentrate on the better game. On this particular day, one more in a very disappointing season, Northwestern fell to the Ohio State Buckeyes 12-0, and Wisconsin dropped their homecoming game against Purdue 14-0. In the meantime, Art and Bryce noted glumly, Michigan won their fourth game in a row, whipping Chicago 28-0 and remaining undefeated.

Thelma and Alma affected interest in the games, but wisely cheered for no one in particular. The ladies thus retained the gentlemen's undying affection. Everyone knew, of course, that after the broadcasts were over, the real fun and games would begin!

That evening, after a fine dinner at Song Wu's Chinese Restaurant, Hollister broached a suggestion to Wilkinson. "Bryce, I'd like to bounce an idea off of you, so to speak. I know that you want, actually need, something to keep you occupied here in TNW. You have a real go-getter personality, and I'm sure that when you take on a project, you follow through and make certain that things are done right. At any rate, the little talent hunt after last Wednesday's unit meeting got me thinking. There must be literally thousands of former musicians here in TNW who would welcome the opportunity to continue with music. Obviously, there will be others who had all the music they could face in their last lives, and want no more of it.

"My thought is that, with the full approval of whoever has to authorize such a thing, you could undertake a search for accomplished musicians of all types. Once you uncovered a sufficient pool of interested individuals, you could oversee the organization of whatever musical groups seemed appropriate."

Wilkinson grabbed Hollister's suggestion like a hungry shark seizing a fat tuna. "Art, I have absolutely no musical ability myself, but I certainly appreciate a wide variety of music. This kind of project, which could take months or even years, is just the sort of thing I could get my teeth into. I'll look into it right away, provided I can use the three of you as sounding boards from time to time."

"Bryce," said Alma, "I think Art has a great idea there. I'm no musician, but I sure enjoy music. I'd like to become involved in the project, too. You're sure to need help from time to time, and I volunteer to be your number one helper."

"You have my full support, too," said Thelma. Although Art and I will sometimes be involved in Social Committee business, there will be many times I'll be free to help you, too. I suspect it will be the same for Art. Right, Art?"

"I'll certainly help out when I can," said Hollister, "but this will be Bryce's project, not mine. One thing we'll soon be facing is a long stretch without Saturday afternoon football. We can always start our monthly powwows with some discussion of Bryce's project before we, ahem, get on with other things. Tell you what, let's all go back to Bryce's room, and talk about this a bit more."

Back in Wilkinson's room, Thelma asked: "Art, I suspect you have some other project planned for yourself. Can you share it with us?"

"Right you are, doll," Hollister replied, "I've got an immediate scheme in mind, and a long range one as well. In due time all three of you will probably hear more than you care to about both of them. At our next official conclave, two days after Thanksgiving, I promise you all a full report on my first idea. The second one could take me as long as 50 or 60 years, so there's hardly a rush. I never like to toot my own horn too loudly until there's really something to toot it about.

"Now, Bryce, let's talk about your project a bit. I'm going to offer a few comments about certain aspects I'd work on if the project were mine. I'm sure Thelma and Alma will have some worthwhile suggestions as well. After that, it will be time for you to grab the ball and run with it.

"Assuming the project had been properly cleared, I'd have my All Purpose Card endorsed so that I could gain entry to, say, 20 buildings. I'd try to learn which 20 buildings might offer excellent prospecting. I'd bear in mind that I'd need musical experts, such as music teachers, band and orchestra leaders, symphonic conductors and the like to help screen candidates. With at least one helper, presumably Alma, I'd visit one rooming unit after another, having set up appointments ahead of time. I'd do all that with my right hand, while with my left hand I'd seek out accommodations for rehearsals, information on where and when the various groups might perform, and so on.

"Before doing any of this, however, I'd make sure that the Great Minds themselves approved the idea, and would make musical instruments available to all who needed them."

Even before Hollister finished his remarks, Wilkinson had turned on his computer, booted up a word processing program, and begun to take notes. As the evening and conversation wore on, Bryce made more and more notes.

Hollister made plans to meet Wilkinson for a late breakfast in the morning, then asked Thelma if she'd care to sleep with him in his own room that night. Thelma accepted, and they both bid Bryce and Alma good night.

After their breakfast the next morning, Hollister suggested that Wilkinson get his feet wet, and call Stanley Caldwell's office on Monday, requesting a joint appointment for himself and Hollister. That way they could both exchange ideas with Caldwell at the same time, and see what help and encouragement they received. For each man, this would be a first attempt to make a contribution to the part of TNW which lay beyond the building in which he lived.

On Tuesday afternoon, Hollister met briefly with Wilkinson, and asked how he had made out in setting up the appointment with Caldwell. Wilkinson reported that the appointment was set for Tuesday, November 8th, at 9:00 a.m., and that Caldwell would make the whole morning available to them if they needed it. Promising to see each other at the Halloween party that night, the two men went their separate ways.

The Halloween festivities in Unit 414 began about 7:30 that night, and the costumes were something to behold! There were witches, pirates, various animals, a gypsy prince and princess, an aviator, and a number of exotic garments which defied exact classification, but were delightful to behold. The residents of Units 413 and 414 had obviously gone to great effort to outdo each other, but everyone agreed that Nina Stivers took the cake!

Characterizing Lady Godiva, Nina wore a long platinum blonde wig and a smile. And, she carefully wore her borrowed tresses hanging down behind her, so as not to obstruct anyone's view. There were a few collisions among the party goers, when someone catching sight of Nina for the first time became distracted and didn't watch his or her step, but the only casualties were a few spilled drinks.

One of the first things that caught Hollister's eye was a piano. Bryce Farnsworth had obviously been busy and persuasive in arranging to have the piano delivered for use at the party. As Hollister took note of the great job his fellow member of the Social Committee had done in organizing the party, Farnsworth came up to him.

"Evening, Art," Farnsworth began. "You know, I tried to get Nina to do a strip for all the guests tonight, as part of the entertainment. She turned me down, saying that it wouldn't be appropriate, and not offering any further explanation. Now I see what she meant! Nina did, by the way, say she'd be happy to perform for us sometime soon, perhaps on New Year's Eve."

"I'll look forward to that, Clayton," Hollister interjected. "Now, before we go on, I want to commend you on your party preparations. The decorations are great, the snacks and drinks are terrific—I particularly enjoyed the hot cider and donuts—and I see you even got hold of a piano."

"That's right, Art, and in a few minutes you and I are going to play and sing for the people. I'll start out with a couple of solos, then take a break to talk with the crowd for a few minutes. After that, if it's okay with you, we'll let the guests make requests. You can play, and we'll all sing along if we can get the group in the mood. We don't have any real booze to prime the pump, as it were, but I'm sure we'll get along just fine anyhow."

"Thanks for all the advance notice, Clayton. Luckily, I've often been called upon to play in situations more or less like this, and I foresee no problems."

About twenty minutes later, Farnsworth took the rostrum and first gestured, then called for quiet. The din dulled to a whisper, and Farnsworth began to speak.

"Good evening, ladies and gentlemen, and Happy Halloween! We're delighted to have our neighbors from Unit 413 here with us tonight, and we hope you're all enjoying yourselves. I'm Clayton Farnsworth, your official host for the evening. My friend Art Hollister and I will entertain you with a couple of musical numbers, then I'll be back to conduct a very small musical survey among our guests from Unit 413. After that, we'll entertain requests from the audience, hopefully for songs most of us know so we can all join in singing."

In a low voice, Farnsworth told Hollister the names of three show tunes he hoped to sing, two as his main offering and one as an encore if the crowd seemed to want one. Hollister was familiar with all the songs, and on a nod from Farnsworth, he began to play. Farnsworth's rich baritone voice enthralled his audience, Hollister's accompaniment was perfect, and the pair were resoundingly called on for an encore. Then, as planned, they took a break.

"Now," said Farnsworth to the crowd, "I'd like to take a brief poll of our guests from Unit 413. How many of you were, in your last lives, either professional musicians or very accomplished amateurs. And also, were any of you band leaders, choir directors, orchestra directors or music teachers? Will any of you who fit those categories, and who might be interested in becoming involved in musical endeavors here in TNW, please raise your hands?"

When four guests raised their hands, Clayton asked them all to get together with him after the songfest. The singing went on for close to an hour, then drew to a close only when Farnsworth and Hollister insisted. Out of some twenty requests, Hollister had only been stumped once.

While indulging in more cider, donuts and other snacks, Hollister and Farnsworth sat with the four guests who had raised their hands. Farnsworth asked the guests to introduce themselves, and to describe briefly what areas of music had held their interests during their recently completed lives on Earth.

"I'm Roy Johnston," said the first man, "and I was a country fiddler. I'm dressed like a hillbilly tonight because that's pretty much what I was. I played at square dances, hoedowns, weddings, barn raisings and all manner of parties, all over Madison County, Tennessee."

"I'm Verna Schultz," said a lady who just seemed to ooze competence, and was dressed like a Circus Ringmaster. "I was a high school music teacher in Brookside Park, Delaware. I directed the mixed chorus at the school, and the best church choir in town, too."

"I'm Hans Hilmer," said a man wearing a gladiator costume. "I played flute in the Cincinnati Symphony for 18 years."

"I'm Carlos Sanchez," said a caballero in a handsome Mexican style outfit. "I played in a Mariachi band in San Diego, mostly trumpet and sometimes guitar."

Farnsworth, who had been taking notes as the musicians introduced themselves, thanked the quartet and said he'd keep in touch with them. Hollister later told Farnsworth about Bryce Wilkinson's intended project, and asked him whether he'd be interested in working with Bryce. Farnsworth answered in the affirmative.

As the witching hour approached, Farnsworth called for the group's attention one last time. Now, my friends, it's time to present the Unit 413/414 Trophy for Best Dressed-Halloween Party Goer for 1933. It really should have read Best-Undressed, since the winner this year, by unanimous vote of the judges, is Nina Stivers!"

A roar of applause, and not a few whistles, greeted Nina as she accepted her prize, her eyes sparkling.

Four days later the occupants of Unit 414 were gathered together to say good-bye to Sandra Richards. This was strictly a white tie, full-dress formal occasion for the men. Since their computers could supply any kind of outfits they wished, the women wore lavish gowns, gorgeous fur wraps and a profusion of diamonds and other jewels. Fantasy or not, the ladies really got into the spirit of things.

After an excellent dinner, featuring all of Sandra's favorite pseudofoods, Barney Rickley, Master of Ceremonies, stood to address the gathering.

"Hello there folks, and welcome to our special send-off for Sandra Richards, a very special lady. Had it not been for Sandy, someone else would have had to baby sit us this past month! Seriously, Sandy, you've done a great job. At least we now have some idea of what we're doing here, and how to enjoy it. I know this has been a strain on you. When we first got here you looked about 30, and now, a month later, you look at least—".

At that point, Rickley clamped his right hand over his own mouth in feigned distress.

"No, Sandy, I'm not going to make age jokes at your expense, even if you have been a dear old grey-haired mother to us! My best writers are still back on Earth, and you know I'll keep on milking that excuse for all it's worth. At any rate, I'll keep this short and sweet.

"You have done a wonderful job getting us going and organized, Sandra, and we want to thank you wholeheartedly. Rather than giving you a lavish gift that would disappear as soon as you went outside the building, we have created this special Thank You card, signed by all of us and encased in a special envelope which will, we've been assured by those who should know, protect this card as long as you wish to keep it."

With that, Rickley turned to Sandra, handed her the card and gave her a big kiss.

Sandra arose, turned to the crowd, and with tears in her eyes and an almost timid-sounding voice, thanked everyone. Hating anti-climaxes, Sandra had turned to leave the room when a voice behind her said "Hey, lady. Wanna play 'You Show Me Yours and I'll Show You Mine?' "

The next morning, when Hollister awoke, Sandra was gone. There was, however, a note on her pillow:

> Dear Art,
>   It was very sweet of you to invite me to spend my last night in Unit 414 with you, and I enjoyed every minute of it. Would you believe that yours was the first proposition I received in all the time I spent with your group? I was afraid I was losing my touch! Maybe we'll run into each other again sometime.
>   Warmest Best Wishes, Sandy

Chapter 12

As they approached the Main Administration building for their appointment with Stanley Caldwell, Hollister and Wilkinson noted that their destination was just next door to Central Processing, a place they remembered well.

Both men were pleased to note that they became clothed as soon as they entered the building, and that their special briefcases, which they had drawn from General Supply in Building KK 280, seemed intact. Everyone inside the Main Administration Building was fully clothed, leading Bryce and Art to the conclusion that when TNW residents needed dignity, they got it. The building itself was clean, apparently well organized, and not terribly different from many office buildings on Earth.

An elevator whisked both men to the tenth floor, where a receptionist directed them to Caldwell's office. Caldwell greeted both men in a friendly fashion, invited them into his private office, and offered them comfortable seating.

"Well, gentlemen, what can I do for you?" Caldwell inquired.

"I," said Wilkinson, "have a project I'd like to discuss with you. For all I know, similar projects may have taken place all over TNW, very likely some are underway now. Nonetheless, what I have in mind will be of immeasurable benefit to people here.

"By the way, I'm a little confused on how we souls here in TNW should refer to each other. I'm so used to using men, women, people, him, her, he, she, they, guys, girls, gals, buddies, bodies and so on. Is there really any harm in doing that? Can it cause any problems?"

"All of us really feel that way," replied Caldwell. "That's the way we were used to alluding to living, or dead, people on Earth, and that's how we refer to them here. Use whatever speech forms you are comfortable with, and don't worry about it. Now, what's your proposed project?"

"It's something we've already tested out in two adjoining units on the 4th floor of Building KK 280. Recognizing what an enriching, entertaining and soul satisfying thing music was for people on Earth, we polled just two rooming units, a total of only 32 souls, to see how many of those had been reasonably accomplished musicians on Earth. We found eight individuals with strong musical backgrounds who were interested in getting involved in music here in TNW. That represented 25% of everybody we asked.

"What I'd like now is your authorization to poll the residents of just four buildings, mine and three adjacent ones, and find out how much interest there is in things musical. Once we tabulate the results, chances are we'll want to expand our efforts to, say, 20 units selected from all over TNW. In any event, we'll work closely with the Wonderful Central Processor staff. We'll report our findings to the TNW administration, along with suggestions on where we might go from there.

"Before I do anything more, however, I want positive assurance that musical instruments will be available to all musicians who need them."

"All right, Bryce, that's a very interesting idea. Now, Art, what's on your mind?"

"Very simply put, Stan, I want to become one of the major movers and shakers here in TNW. Precisely, I want to become Special Projects Director."

"You don't beat around the bush, do you, Art," Caldwell remarked.

"No, Stan, I don't. When I've determined a course of action, I get on with it. Whoever has the responsibility I'm talking about simply isn't doing the job, regardless of who he or she is, or was

"I want six months to learn a great deal more about TNW, to travel all over this place, to visit with the Great Minds, to talk with a wide cross section of souls, learn about the history of TNW, and find out how the place really works. At the end of that six months, I'll be as ready as a soul could ever be to take over the position of Special Projects Director.

"As I have it figured, I'll engage an Associate Director immediately. That person and I will then build a staff of a dozen top assistants, each with expertise in a particular area. In addition, we'll take on whatever clerical help we need. Special project ideas, after initial screening by ombudsmen like yourself, will be fed to our office. Probably 90% of the ideas will either be rejected by us, or provisionally accepted. The provisionally accepted ideas will be tested. If they prove out, the projects will be scheduled for appropriate implementation. The rest will be shelved.

"The Special Projects Office will routinely report to the Great Minds on test projects, and on those it has approved for implementation. When something comes along that could be TNW-shaking, that proposal will be promptly forwarded to the Great Minds for disposition. In other words, we'll pass the hot potatoes along at once!

"Before implementing any project initially developed by the office itself, the Special Projects Office will always request prior Great Minds approval.

"Here's a copy of my proposal, Stan, with my name, address and phone number on it. I believe that's a copy of his proposal Bryce is handing you now. Please get back to us as soon as possible, after the Great Minds have either accepted or rejected these offers."

On that note, Hollister and Wilkinson shook hands with Caldwell and left his office.

Hollister made only one comment as the two made their way out of the building. "That's my philosophy, Bryce. Dazzle 'em with footwork and get the hell out. Now all we can do is wait."

A week later, word came to Hollister and Wilkinson that Stanley Caldwell wanted to see them. Their appointment was set for 9:00 a.m. on Thursday, and they were to hold the whole morning open. Sensing a need to confer with each other, the two met in the kitchen, where they decided to sin a bit as they talked. Each one selected a delicious looking slice of pie, and both took cups of coffee well-laced with cream. They carried their snacks across to the dining room, and sat down to enjoy both food and conversation.

"So, Bryce," said Hollister, "what do you think Caldwell will tell us?"

"If I had to make book on it," Wilkinson replied, "I'd say that they have approved my suggested project, since it is limited in scope and relatively harmless. You, on the other hand, have proposed something of much greater magnitude. They'll admire your spirit, but stop short of giving you a blank check"

"You're probably right on both counts," Hollister said. "I may have come on a bit strong. But, when I get enthused about something, that's my way. Anyhow, on Thursday we'll know—it says here."

Thursday came in a hurry, and once more Hollister and Wilkinson were seated in Caldwell's office. After a few pleasantries, the three men got down to business.

"I've got good news for you, Bryce," said Caldwell. "Your suggested project has been approved by the Great Minds. They consider what you propose to undertake to be of manageable size, and wish you well. Feel free to confer with the Wonderful Central Processor staff for whatever help you need. They will be expecting to hear from you.

"And, to relieve your mind, TNW Central Supply can supply whatever instruments your musicians require. All the musicians have to do is order what they need through the General Supply Office in their own building. The instruments are all of high quality, and come with carrying cases in which they can be safely transported anywhere in TNW.

"Now, Art, we come to your plan. While the Great Minds admire your willingness to take on the job which you call 'Special Projects Director,' they wonder whether you fully understand what you could be getting yourself into. The Great Minds noted that one of the many preliminary steps you intended to take was a visit with them. They are all for such a meeting, and your appointment with them is in ten minutes!"

"Holy mackerel, Stan, nothing like giving a guy a lot of advance notice!"

"Art, if you're half the man I think you are, you'll have no trouble. I'm not necessarily predicting that the Great Minds will soon be eating out of your hand, but then, who knows?"

"Stan, do you mind, or will the Great Minds mind, if I take Bryce along with me to the meeting?"

"They specifically mentioned only you, Art, but the Great Minds are adaptable. Your having Bryce with you should present no problem. The Great Minds occupy the entire top floor, that's the 12th floor, of this building. It's been good seeing you again, and good luck to you both!"

Bryce and Art had about five minutes to talk privately before they got on the elevator. How many Great Minds are there, they wondered. Are they entire, human-looking souls, or maybe just detached brains in glass jars of fluid, with wires running out of them to who knows where? Whatever the case, Art & Bryce were about to find out!

The twelfth floor offices were, as Hollister and Wilkinson had expected, a bit more lavish than others they had seen so far in The Next World. Nonetheless, what they found when they were ushered into the conference room surprised them both. The room contained three very normal looking people. One gentleman, wearing wildly checked slacks, a shirt with a bow tie, a vest and a boater hat, was softly and expertly playing a piano in the corner. A second man, wearing a sweater with a big "Y" on it, was reading a publication called "Football Weekly." The third individual, dressed in attire which would have looked correct at a country club, was practicing her putting on the thick, rich carpet.

"Greetings," said the Yale man, "and welcome to our play room. It can't be work, work, work all the time! I, by the by, am Harry Hendricks. This is Olga Olson, and that gent at the piano is Sam Schwartz."

"It's a pleasure to meet you all. I'm Art Hollister, and this is my friend Bryce Wilkinson. We were in the neighborhood, and thought we'd drop in and say hello." Hollister was determined to keep his remarks in the same semi-flippant vein as that in which he had been addressed.

In the same spirit, Wilkinson gave the surprising trio a friendly wave and a smile.

"Okay, folks." said Schwartz, who had left the piano and seated himself at the conference table, "Sit down, both of you, and let's talk. You, Hollister, want to replace Emma Sturdevant, just because she's done nothing to speak of for the last 20 years, and wouldn't know an original idea if it bit her! On the other hand, Wilkinson, that cozy little project you came up with might work out pretty well. I've always liked music, and anything that furthers it gets my vote."

"Tell me, Hollister, aside from being grandiose, and just about making you one of the chiefs around here, of what real value would a Special Projects Director's Office be?" Harry Hendricks asked.

"And what good would all of this do for golf, Hollister?" asked Olga Olson.

"Not much, Miss Olson, since it looks like golf already rides high around here, pardon the mixed metaphor."

"Well," said Olga, "at least the man's not afraid to snap back!"

"Frankly," said Hollister, "I volunteered for the job because I felt I could make a contribution. Just how much I can accomplish, and how much really needs to be accomplished, I won't know until I've found out an awful lot more about TNW. For now, I need your approval, and backing, while I investigate, learn, and see what I can come up with.

"Before we go a lot further, I'll answer a question I know you're dying to ask, if you'll excuse the expression. Namely, what particular pet project would I work on first?

"There seems to be a policy here in TNW which prevents a soul from learning about its past lives, all of those which might have taken place before its most recent one. I've mulled that one over again and again, and can see no reason why such a policy should exist. Can you enlighten me?"

"Truthfully, Hollister," replied Schwartz, "I'm not really sure why we left that taboo in place when we set things up here. Just because, with rare exceptions, humans on Earth remember nothing about any previous lives they may have had, I guess we simply continued things in that vein. How about you, Olga, Harry, what do you think about this?"

Olga and Harry conferred with each other in low tones for a couple of minutes, then Olga replied. "Let's face it, Sam, that one was just tradition. What real harm can come from a soul's learning that he once cut stone as a pyramid builder in Egypt, or drove a chariot in Rome or whatever? Tell you what, Hollister, why don't you and Wilkinson step outside for about fifteen minutes, while the three of us talk this over?"

Art and Bryce nodded, left the office, and spent the next quarter hour chatting with the receptionist, and talking between themselves. When they returned to the Great Minds' office, Sam Schwartz spoke once again, addressing Hollister this time by his first name.

"Art, you've won one already. Take the next week or so to work up a proposal on how you'd disclose past life information to TNW residents. We'll endorse your All Purpose Card so you can talk freely with anyone in Central Processing. By the way, there's a special side entrance to that building that will let you avoid the naked soul routine once you're inside, just as you can here in the Main Administration Building.

"Make an appointment with the receptionist to come back here on the Monday after Thanksgiving, with your proposal. At that time we'll work out how far and how fast you should proceed with this, and perhaps discuss some other matters as well."

Hollister passed his All Purpose Card over to Schwartz, who used a special device to enter the appropriate endorsement, then passed the card back to Hollister. The visitors shook hands with the Great Minds, thanked them and left the office. Art stopped at the reception desk, made his appointment for Monday, November 27th, and re-joined Wilkinson. A few minutes later, thanks to the Ultrasonic Transport System, Hollister and Wilkinson were back in their own rooming unit.

Chapter 13

Hollister used one of the days before Thanksgiving to visit Central Processing, and to chat with one of the administrators in the Wonderful Central Processor Department, Assistant Director Alice Thompson.

"Miss Thompson," Hollister began, "I'm Art Hollister. The Great Minds suggested I drop in and visit your department. Here's my All Purpose Card, which I believe has been properly endorsed."

Thompson took the card, checked it with her scanner, did a sort of double take and returned the card to Hollister. "The Great Minds apparently place a great deal of confidence in you, Mr. Hollister. That's the highest clearance level I've ever seen. In brief, it means that anything you ask me I'm to answer if I can."

"Great," said Hollister. "The first thing I ask is that you call me Art from now on, and I'll call you Alice. I've always done business on a first name basis, and am too set in my ways to change now. Okay?"

"As you wish, Art. Now, how can I help you?"

"Second, I'd like to know how you keep track of all the souls here, and how you can differentiate between all the ones who have the same name."

"That one is amazingly easy, Art. Each soul has an All Purpose Card, as you know, and each card has its own individual code. The same code is embedded in the individual's mind, too, and we have special scanners which can positively identify the codes. We have over 107,000 John Joneses here, and we can tell them all apart."

"Next, Alice, how do you store the information on a soul's past lives. You know, the stuff about what body they were in a hundred or even a thousand years ago?"

"That data is not currently made available to individual souls, except during the soul's personal placement interview. All the information you're talking about, including a one paragraph encapsulation of each former life the soul has had a part in, is specially encrypted on each soul's All Purpose Card. The soul can't read it, but we at Central Processing can.

"You have to remember, too, that some souls here have no past lives, except for the ones they finished just before they came here to TNW. The shortfall between souls needed to occupy the bodies of the newly born, and the number of souls who opt to recycle, increases steadily. To meet the demand, The Wonderful Central Processor
creates more and more fresh new souls each year."

"Alice," Hollister asked, "could you, with proper approval, modify the computer system all over TNW so that a soul could read his prior lives' history on his own computer, and even print it out if he chose to do so? I assume, of course, that a message could be permanently added to every soul's computer bulletin board, telling him that this information could now be obtained?"

"Given the right authorization, we could accomplish that whole process in half an hour or so."

"I suspected as much. Now, Alice, tell me if souls ever wear-out."

"That's an intriguing question, Art. None of the souls we've generated with the Wonderful Central Processor has ever worn out. Some of them have already been recycled several times, having repeatedly had the misfortune to inhabit the bodies of those who died young. Sometimes we come across an old time soul that has recycled thirty times or more, and is still in great shape. On other occasions, we find that a soul which has only recycled half a dozen times or so is not fit for further use on Earth. Fortunately, the Wonderful Central Processor can refurbish those tired souls so they can enjoy their well-earned retirement here in TNW."

"Can the Wonderful Central Processor send a soul backwards and forwards through time, or on temporary visits to Earth, with a subsequent return to TNW? Also, can cargoes be transported in either direction?"

"Some time travel is possible. Given special authorization by the Great Minds, The Wonderful Central Processor can make arrangements for such a trip. The actual equipment for such travel, however, is located in the Enhanced Production Center, across the street next to Central Supply. Travel forward in time a distance of up to 100 years is possible. Travel backwards is limited to return trips to the date from which the traveler started. So now, Art, do you have any other questions?

"Yes I do, Alice. What service currently unavailable from Central Processing do souls most frequently ask you to provide?"

"That's easy. Far more souls would recycle if they had some guarantees about what kind of bodies they would be going into. They aren't looking for guarantees that they'll be beautiful, rich and famous. But, they want such things as a gender guarantee, a skin color guarantee, a general health guarantee and a comfort level guarantee. Roughly 90% of those who were women in their just finished lives want to be women again, while about 95% of male souls want to be men again. Only about 20% of those who were homosexuals want to stay that way in their next lives.

"Close to 100% of those who were caucasian want white skin again, most of the orientals want yellow skin again, while about 80 to 90 percent of those who were black-skinned, brown-skinned, American Indian, Eskimo or members of other minority racial groups would opt to have that color of skin again. Nobody wants to recycle into an existence of grinding poverty, terrible health or both. Nearly everyone would prefer to be part of a culture similar to the one he or she recently left. You could consider that part of the wish for an acceptable comfort level. Presently we can guarantee those who re-cycle the color of skin they want, but that's about all."

"Right now, Alice, I have just one more general inquiry. Can you give me your office phone number, and the codes by which I can reach you via computer, so I can get any further information I may need from you without making a personal visit the next time? Don't get me wrong, this visit has been a pleasure, and I appreciate your help, but there are times when only a quick phone call is necessary."

Alice gave Hollister the data he needed, neatly printed on a 3x5 file card, which was, she assured Hollister, impervious to the hazards of outdoor travel in TNW. Thanking her, Hollister headed home, where he needed all of a leisurely half-hour to put together his proposal for the Great Minds.

Two days later, on Thursday, November 23, 1933, the residents of Unit 414, Building KK 280, observed their first Thanksgiving Day together. They were thankful indeed that they were enjoying the pleasant camaraderie of The Next World, rather than the cold, sterile afterlife of a "heaven", the scalding hot torment of a "hell" or the absolute nothing of simply rotting away. The dinner tasted as fine as anyone could remember from a Holiday dinner on Earth, and the gathering was a complete success.

THE NEXT WORLD

On Saturday, the Frolicsome Four got together for their monthly conclave. Once again the football news was discouraging. Wisconsin lost their season finale to Minnesota, 6 to 3 at Minneapolis, and Northwestern fell to Michigan 13 to 0, in a game played in Evanston. Making things even less bearable was that Michigan completed an undefeated season, marred only by a 0 to 0 tie with Minnesota the previous week, to win the Big Ten Championship. Art and Bryce knew that Clayton Farnsworth would be ecstatic. This could have really depressed the guys, but the fun and games that followed the football broadcasts brightened their day, a lot!

Suddenly it was Monday morning, and Hollister was once again shown into the conference room on the 12th floor of the Main Administration building. Hollister shook hands with everyone, and beat them to the punch by greeting all the Great Minds by their first names, and wishing them all good morning. The Great Minds replied in kind, and the meeting was off to a fine start.

Hollister handed each Great Mind a copy of his proposal, and kept one for himself. He then began his brief and succinct commentary.

"As you see, we can handle this one like a breeze. In less than a half hour after we give Central Processing a 'Go', they can be ready to supply each soul with a brief capsule version of every past life he or she may ever have lived. Some will have lots of past lives, some only one. But, everyone who cares can now have the information, in confidence. If a soul wants to share the story with friends, fine, but the files will be transmitted only to the soul whose All Purpose Card is inserted in a given computer.

"So, any objections?" Hollister paused a few moments, noted no objections whatever, and went on. "Fair enough, I'll count on whichever of you handles that sort of thing to issue the appropriate approval to Central Processing. Now, suppose we chat for a while. I'd really like to learn more about you three, how you came to set up TNW, and all that sort of thing."

"Art," said Harry Hendricks, "we've talked and thought a lot about you since your last visit. You're the kind of guy we knew would show up here sooner or later, and we're glad you did. I think the four of us should spend the next several hours talking over many things, past, present and future. We'll see where we go from there.

"Olga, Sam and I first met at a major, interdisciplinary series of seminars. The meetings were held in Chicago, in the early summer of 1893, in conjunction with the World's Columbian Exhibition. Between the incredible exhibits and the superb scientific presentations we were all taking in, it's amazing we had time or inclination to develop a personal relationship, but develop one we did. From that time on, both on Earth and in our after lives, the three of us have been incredibly close, in both personal and professional matters.

"The three of us were considered to be geniuses of one sort or another, yet we retained practical outlooks. We instinctively knew that all the incredible knowledge in the universe means nothing if you can't apply it."

Olga Olson took up the account. "The three of us lived happily together for the next five years. We discovered that we all had an avid interest in the hereafter, and as an intellectual exercise during that stretch of time we developed our own concept of what a perfect, or close

THE NEXT WORLD

to it, life after death might be like. And that's the kind of set-up we now have here in TNW.

"Brilliant as we were for our time, though, there was no way we could figure out how to bring a place such as TNW into being. We knew what we wanted to create, but had no way to achieve it. It was apparent to us that we'd require a miracle and, yes, we got one.

"In July of 1898, we were living in Massachusetts as a happy trio. To celebrate our fifth anniversary together, and because we all wanted to go anyway, we made plans to attend the Trans-Mississippi Exposition in Omaha, Nebraska. We set out by train for Omaha, only to suffer disaster in Ohio when a railroad bridge collapsed, dumping our pullman car and several others into a deep gorge. The three of us were killed instantly, part of an awesome total of 93 people who lost their lives.

"That was the beginning of our miracle, or rather a series of seeming miracles. When we next became aware of anything, the three of us weren't on our way to hell for living in sin. We didn't know exactly where we were, or whither we were bound. What had happened was that our souls, along with those of all the others who died in that same wreck, were gathered up by what amounted to a giant vacuum cleaner, and brought on board a huge spaceship from the distant Planet Baldaur. The spaceship and its occupants had been in the vicinity of Earth for some time, studying the planet's geography and generally observing life there from a distance.

"Fortuitously, the wreck of our train, and the group of free souls it created, came along just at the time when the crew aboard the craft were ready to use their spirit gathering device for the first time. They had expected to pick up a few souls here and there, but when a whole cluster became available at once they grabbed us all up.

"The charm of the Baldonian's scheme was that they had developed a method by which they could gather and study the minds of deceased humans, their souls as it were, and not disturb the lives of humans on Earth. Their scheme was beautiful, and so were they—not in their physical appearance, but in their outlook on the universe and its inhabitants."

At this point, Sam Schwartz took up the narrative. "When we first became conscious aboard the spaceship, we were all naked souls, just like the mobs of souls who move through Central Processing here in TNW every day. So as not to startle or alarm us unduly, the Baldonians had assumed exactly the same appearance. In fact, to this day we don't know what they look like when they are among themselves.

"The Baldonians' giant vacuum had gathered up a few odd artifacts from Earth along with their catch of souls. There was a book, a lady's head scarf, a man's derby hat, a fountain pen and a few other odds and ends. While most of the Baldonians present were examining the collection of miscellaneous items, one of their number came toward our group, carrying something which looked sort of like a cross between a shotgun and a baseball bat. The Baldonian began talking to us in a language totally unknown to any of us, then pointed the thing he was carrying at one of our heads, and pushed a switch on its side. The device let out a loud hum for about a minute, then fell silent when the Baldonian touched the switch again.

"The Baldonian began speaking again, this time in perfect English. He explained that we were aboard the spaceship *Arcturan* from the Planet Baldaur, that all of us would be the guests of the Baldonians for a stretch of time, that the Baldonians meant us no harm, and that his name was Zindar. Having scanned one of us, the Baldonians would now be able to communicate with us in our language. They were here to study Planet Earth, just as they and their counterparts aboard other spaceships had studied many other planets over an extended period of time.

"Taking up, one by one, the group of rather mundane items the giant Baldonian vacuum had sucked in along with us souls, Zindar asked us to explain what they were. I happened to be sitting near our host, and did my best to answer his questions. I explained that a derby was a man's hat, and showed Zindar how it was worn. I identified the lady's head scarf, and Olga modeled that for Zindar.

"I examined the book, found that it was *The Innocents Abroad,* by Mark Twain, and explained that books were a means by which humans communicated ideas, both truthful and fictional, by use of the printed word. This particular book, I commented, was a whimsical and satirical account of a trip Twain had made to Europe and the Holy Land. Actual facts were mixed with deft humor, all in a style that had made Twain one of America's most popular authors.

"By writing briefly on a back flyleaf of the book, I showed Zindar how a fountain pen worked.

"I met my biggest challenge when Zindar found a tin box of rubber condoms among the collection of stuff, and asked me what they were. I replied that they were devices used to control both human population and human disease, and let it go at that.

"The first real indication we had that the Baldonians were going to be a 'fun' group was when they reproduced the scarf and derby, and all began wearing one or the other. Zindar explained that this would help the naked souls from the train wreck tell themselves apart from the simulated souls who were actually Baldonians. What impressed me was how quickly and easily the Baldonians had made the copies. If they could make hats and scarves out of nothing, and in almost no time at all, what else could they make?"

Chapter 14

It was time for a break, and to Hollister's delight, the Great Mind's obviously knew how to do it in style. The room to which the four adjourned was truly set up right. There were coffee, tea, and hot chocolate to choose from for hot beverages, chilled orange juice, grapefruit juice, pineapple juice, grape juice and tomato juice, bacon and pork sausages, an assortment of delicious sweet rolls, and a virtual mountain of fresh donuts. There may not have been salaries for the volunteers who worked for the TNW administration, but there were obviously some dandy fringe benefits! It was wonderful, thought Hollister, that you could stuff yourself with goodies like this and never gain an ounce. Topping things off, there were no medical problems like diabetes, high blood pressure or heart disease to put a damper on things, and keep doctors busy. Doctors could play golf every day if the wished to do so!

After the quartet returned to the conference room, Harry Hendricks continued the story of the time the trio and their fellow souls had spent aboard the Baldonian Spaceship. "As time went on, every soul who had died in that train wreck was interviewed several times. In addition, the Baldonians used a powerful combination scanner/recorder to record the mind contents of each soul. They soon learned to sort out and discard the mundane drivel from these recordings, and to save the worthwhile knowledge the minds had contained. The recording process itself took only a few minutes per soul, and was entirely harmless to the soul's mind. Like every other experience the souls had aboard the Arcturan, the recording sessions were completely painless.

"From the beginning, Zindar was our main contact among the Baldonians. Soon it became a case of our interviewing him as much as he was interviewing us. It happened that I had been a leading authority on all kinds of world history—geological, geographical, military, political, mechanical, artistic, you name it. If you didn't have an encyclopedia handy, or the one you had was lacking, you called Harry Hendricks. This particular wealth of historical knowledge was the kind of thing the Baldonians were looking for, and I offered to help them organize a history of Planet Earth that would be far superior to any recording they could make from my mind alone. This offer was one of our biggest bargaining chips, since it soon became apparent that the Baldonians could help us, a lot. I'll let Olga take over the story here, and tell you how she made a marvelous contribution."

"One of my chief areas of study," Olga began, "had been in the area of human persuasion. It was a challenge to me to see whether we could influence alien minds, those of the Baldonians, using techniques we had found effective on humans. Above all else, we were honest with Zindar. We all pitched in to explain that we had dreamed of creating a system of afterlife for human souls that would be far superior to any which souls had known before. We knew, in large part, what sort of place we wanted to set up and operate. Unfortunately, we didn't know how to do it. We wanted to have all the facilities and amenities that TNW now offers, plus a few others which ultimately proved impractical.

"We needed a means of channeling all newly-deceased souls to our facility, and a means of rapidly and efficiently processing them when they got there. We needed the ability to travel, rapidly and safely, backwards and forwards through time. We had to be able to bring cargoes of certain things back to TNW from Earth, and to build from plans and materials samples, reproducing buildings and the like perfectly and virtually instantaneously. When necessary, we had to be able to up-date existing facilities very rapidly.

"Although souls don't really need food, we wanted to give them an endless supply of what seemed to be food and drink, yet not have the bother of disposal of bodily wastes. Since eating and sex are two of a human's greatest pleasures, we wanted souls here in TNW to have all they wanted of both.

"In short, we wanted all sorts of things, and we asked the Baldonians to help us achieve them. To our great delight, they agreed. Having explored vast portions of the universe, the Baldonians knew a perfect spot for establishing The Next World. Sight unseen, we accepted their suggested location. It's difficult to explain exactly where it is, but that hardly matters, does it? Suffice it to say, this site for TNW has worked out perfectly.

"We asked the Baldonians to review their recordings
of the minds of all the souls who had come aboard the spaceship with us, with an eye to seeing if some of those souls might be particularly helpful to us in getting our project off the ground, so to speak.

"To our amazement, four of the souls were those of a group of architects who had been on their way back home after attending a convention in New York. One was a specialist in municipal and manufacturing buildings, one was an expert on large apartment buildings, a third was a wizard at all sorts of structural engineering and the fourth was superb at building interior layout and decoration. The four men had all been members of the same Chicago firm, and had worked together on many projects. We set out at once to persuade those four souls to join our team, and help us create TNW.

"We set up a meeting between the four architects, Zindar and ourselves. At that get together we explained briefly what we intended to do, and asked the architects for their help. Three of them agreed readily, but the interiors expert, who had been a super clean-living devout Catholic during his lifetime, expressed serious doubts. He figured he had a guaranteed spot in heaven awaiting him, and he wanted to meet Saint Peter at the Gate as soon as possible. We finally induced the interiors expert, whose name was Timothy O'Rourke, to work with us in the design phases of our project, and take things a step further and collaborate in the actual construction and decorating of our first buildings.

"In exchange, we promised to eventually turn Tim, and any other souls aboard the Spaceship who wished it, loose as free spirits to find their ways to heaven or hell or wherever. We ourselves were not convinced that those places existed, but in TNW's earliest days we weren't the processors of all souls as we are today.

"In a series of further meetings, we talked with all the other souls aboard the spaceship, told them what we were up to, and invited them to join us. All but two of the other souls excitedly agreed to join us for the long haul. Talk about a resurgence of the American pioneer spirit!

"The Baldonians were on no fixed time schedule, and for the next 17 months or so they helped us set up and fine tune TNW, in preparation for our Grand Opening on January 1, 1900. Our group of pioneer souls, all of whom occupied apartments in Building A 1, volunteered to fill various reception and processing jobs as we got under way.

"Before they left us, our Baldonian friends set up the equivalent of a two-way radio system by which we could contact them from time to time, and call for help if we needed it.

"On December 29, 1899 we said good-bye to Zindar, all the other Baldonians, and the three souls who had elected not to be a part of TNW. We thanked everyone for their help, wished them well, and waved as the spaceship *Arcturan* departed. In three days The Next World would officially open for business!"

"I guess it's my turn for a while," said Sam Schwartz. "In the center of things, we put together four buildings to handle logistical support for TNW. These are Central Processing, Central Supply, Enhanced Production and Main Administration. We're in business 34 years now, and those buildings are still half empty. Our whole idea was to hold down bureaucracy to a minimum.

"On Earth, Man spends his whole life dealing with problems. Some he solves by himself, for some he goes to various experts such as doctors, lawyers, builders and
dozens more you could name. In many cases, man's answer to problems is more government, more workers, more expense. Some agencies go on for years, long after the problems they were set up to work on have been solved, have disappeared or have ceased to be important.

"Here, as I'm sure you have already gathered, we have simply eliminated the problems, at least most of the big ones. Residents are left with choices, however. They have momentous decisions to make, such as what radio program to listen to, what book to read, what subject to paint, what golf course to play and so on. Since we have almost no real problems to solve, we have almost no bureaucracy. Most matters that do come up are handled by the various building administrators, and very few of them ever come before us. Neat, huh?

"And now, Art, let's get to your case. You want to be named Special Projects Director, set up an office full of helpers, and then what? Most of the time you'd have nothing to do, and the boredom would drive you bonkers.

"As we hinted before, we already have a lady named Emma Sturdevant on our staff. Emma, who was one of the original souls from the train wreck, holds the title of New Ideas Chairman. In the early years, Emma actually came up with some interesting suggestions, hers and those of others, and a number of them were incorporated into the TNW set-up.

"Now, Emma doesn't even have an office here. She calls in once a month for messages, and that's about it. In a normal year we see Emma once, at the Central Administration Midwinter Holiday Party. If Emma ever again comes up with something new and interesting, we'll certainly consider it. In the meantime, Emma has her dignity, our thanks for past services rendered, and time to enjoy what amounts to a well-earned retirement.

"What we'd like to do, Art, is make you one of the Great Minds in all but name. If you really want a title, dream one up and it's yours. You'll have free and complete access to everything and everyone in TNW. Whenever there's something noteworthy or urgent up for consideration, we'll call you in for your voice and your vote. When you bring a matter to us, you are assured of full and prompt attention. There's only one more thing we have to be sure of."

"And that is?" asked Hollister.

"Why," interjected Olga Olson, "it's whether or not you play golf."

"I have been known to swing a club," replied Hollister, who in his prime had consistently shot in the mid-seventies.

"Then the matter is settled," said Schwartz. "It's time to adjourn this meeting and have a drink or two. In honor of our new colleague, and the fact that we'll finally have a golf foursome, we'll pour some of our finest simulated Scotch. You'll swear it's really *The Glenlivet!*"

Chapter 15

Back in his room, Hollister used his computer for a few moments, made a notation on a scratch pad, turned off the computer and made a telephone call. When his party answered, Hollister was glad he was sitting down, because he suddenly felt weak in the knees!

"Amy, this is Art."

"Art! I'm so pleased you called. Some women would scold their men unmercifully in a situation like this—we've been dead almost 2 months and you haven't gotten in touch. But you know me better than that. You have no doubt been just as busy getting used to life here in TNW as I have, and besides, I could just as easily have picked up the phone and called you. Come to think of it, this has been just about the right waiting period. When can I see you?"

"Amy, my sweet, I look forward to that just as much as I expect you do. Before I called, I stopped past the office here in my building, which is number KK 280 by the way, and made tentative arrangements for you to visit me here beginning December 14th, and staying until the 21st. Can you fit that into your schedule?"

"You know I can, Art. That means we'll be together on the 20th for Midwinter Holiday!"

"That's right, my dear, and I'll be taking you to a very special party on the 15th as well. I have some wonderful news to share with you, but let's save that until I see you."

"We both have a lot to catch up on, Art. And, oh my, isn't the sex here wonderful? I can hardly wait to get in bed with you again!"

"The desire is mutual, Amy. I'll look forward to your arrival at, say, about mid-morning on the 14th. As I mentioned, my building is number KK 280. My unit number is 414, my room number is 8, and my phone number is 80 953 76 4400. See you soon!"

"You can count on it, Art," said Amy, just before she hung up the phone.

In what seemed like almost no time at all it was the 14th, and Hollister was holding Amy Lawrence in his arms for the first time since the night they had both died, in a fiery explosion at Hollister's Evanston home. Finally the two broke their clinch and gazed at each other. When last together, on Earth, Hollister had been 59 years old, while Amy had been 54. Both had been wracked with cancer, with only a short and painful time to live had nature taken its normal course.

Now, appearing in their prime, Hollister seemed about 30 and Amy a gorgeous 24. Yes, indeed, they both thought, life in TNW had a lot to be said for it! Without further ado, Amy and Art proceeded to Hollister's room, where for the next three hours they enjoyed themselves making love more proficiently and frequently than they had ever managed together back on Earth. Finally they came up for air.

"Well, Art," said Amy languidly, "I see you haven't forgotten how to do it."

"Nor you either, Amy," was Hollister's brief and happy reply.

Their discussion eventually expanded to a declared understanding that during their twice-a-year get togethers, once at Winter Holiday time and once around the Fourth of July, all topics would be open for conversation between them, except for their sexual adventures in TNW. In line with TNW protocol, no form of jealousy would mar their special relationship, whether they were together or apart.

of jealousy would mar their special relationship, whether they were together or apart.

After finally emerging from bed and getting dressed, Art and Amy talked and talked.

Eventually Hollister said, "Amy, I promised you some exciting news, so here goes. I've become acquainted with the Great Minds, the folks who set this place up to begin with, and I'll be working with them. My initial request was to be made a director of special projects, but it got way beyond that. I'll be sort of a chief troubleshooter for the Great Minds. I'll have access to everything and everybody here in TNW, and in general I'll have all the challenges that any soul could want."

"So you couldn't just sit by and accept an eternity's worth of retirement?"

"I guess I'm just not made that way, babe. The beauty of what I'll be doing, though, is that I can proceed at my own pace. Some years I may not do much of anything, while during other stretches of time I'll probably be working pretty hard. Sooner or later I expect to make one or more trips back to Earth, mainly on TNW business. There are a couple of long range projects I'm kicking around in my mind, and as they take shape I'll let you know more about them."

"And so, Art, what have you already done for TNW, and what's next?"

"Well, Amy, I did manage to get one idea adopted. From now on, any soul who wants to know about his or
her past lives, if any, will be able to find out about them.

"Expanding the special projects idea, I'm planning to feel the pulse of the population here, at least a small part of it, and see what ideas a cross section of souls comes up with. I'll ask each individual who cares to participate to or whatever. We'll sort out the practical ideas, and from those choose a few to actually try out."

"Sounds like you have a full plate already, Art. That past lives information center, or whatever you choose to call it, will probably appeal to a lot of souls, at least those who have always been curious about their own earlier lives. Many are doomed to disappointment, though, when they learn that they had only the lives they led just before they came to TNW. Others will be dismayed by how dreary and humdrum some or all of their previous lives were. I mean, when you check on your past expecting to have once been a queen or at least a duchess, and discover that in your most noteworthy life you were a scullery maid or a tavern slut, that's going to be an awful letdown.

"You may be opening a Pandora's Box when you look for special project ideas, but if you start out by asking a relatively small number of souls for suggestions, and promise no one that their ideas will actually be transformed into reality, you'll probably be all right. Whatever you do, don't let the multitudes find out how to call you at home. They'd give you no peace!"

"I've already considered that one, Amy. Souls making suggestions will be able to call the message center at the TNW Main Administration building, or leave written proposals at their building offices, to be forwarded to my office."

"So, lover, with what other things about TNW do you expect to concern yourself?"

"I want to find out what real problems concern the Great Minds, whether those problems involve present practices and policies here in TNW, or whether their roots are back on Earth. If some of these troubling matters involve the Earth and its people, I want to know if TNW can and should help. As time goes on, through involve the Earth and its people, I want to know if TNW can and should help. As time goes on, through discussions with the Great Minds and others, I expect to get a real handle on things.

"On a more mundane level, tonight at dinner you'll meet all the other residents of Unit 414, and a delightful group they are. And, starting about four tomorrow afternoon, we'll be attending that special party I promised you. You'll have an opportunity to meet Harry Hendricks, Olga Olson and Sam Schwartz, something not many residents here get a chance to do."

"And just who are Hendricks, Olson and Schwartz? They sound like partners in a law firm, or maybe a comedy team?"

"Please show a little respect, my dear. Hendricks, Olson and Schwartz are the Great Minds! Luckily you were a fairly decent golfer in your day, so if the talk gets around to the trio's favorite subject you should be able to hold your own. Just tell them about the day you met Gene Sarazen and got his autograph—that ought to impress them! Oh, one other thing, don't ask about their spouses and/or children. These three were a closely knit trio on Earth, if you get my drift, and they still are here in TNW. They never had any children, just as you and I never did."

"Okay, Art, I'll be respectful, but I bet those three are really pretty interesting, and fun at parties, too. I look forward to meeting them."

"One thing I'll say, Amy, is that if the quality of the enhanced continental breakfast those folks provided at the Administration Building the other day is any indication, their Annual Midwinter Holiday party, which I gather they always hold on the Friday before the big day itself, should be a real shindig!"

THE NEXT WORLD

At dinner that night, Art introduced Amy to all the residents of unit 414, and they shared a table with Bryce Wilkinson, Clayton Farnsworth, Thelma Smithback and Alma Norton. They talked about a wide range of subjects, but inevitably the discussion got around to football.

"All right, Clayton, who do you like in the Rose Bowl game?" Hollister asked.

"I frankly couldn't care less, Art. Columbia versus Stanford, east against west, who cares? If they'd only let Big Ten teams play in that game, I'd get excited about it in a hurry—especially since my alma mater seems to win the Big Ten championship rather often. Michigan played in the first Rose Bowl game, back in 1902, and walloped Stanford 49 to 0. That shook the troops on the west coast up so badly that they didn't hold a Rose Bowl football game again until 1916. Whatever the reason, Big Ten teams don't get invited to that game anymore."

"I'd like to see Big Ten teams in that game, too," Wilkinson declared. "Maybe my dear old Badgers would make the grade some year, even though they haven't won a Big Ten championship in football since 1912. By the way, Clayton, I know the Wolverines won the Big Ten championship in 1933, but how do you expect them to do next year?"

"Well, uh, you can always expect Michigan to be in the thick of things!"

"You sound just a mite uncertain for a change," Hollister commented.*

Farnsworth had good cause to hedge his prediction. Michigan lost all but one of its football games in 1934, ending up at the bottom of the Big Ten Conference.

"Boy," said Amy. "You gentlemen seem to take your football pretty seriously. But then, why not? You've got all the time in The Next World to follow your favorite teams, or whatever."

"And as we all know," chimed in Thelma, "the whatever is pretty good here, too!"

Thelma's comment brought general laughter but, fortunately for the slightly nervous Hollister, no general discussion of sex in TNW ensued.

The party the next afternoon, celebrating the forthcoming Midwinter Holiday, was everything Hollister had expected. The decorations were wonderful, the drinks delightful, and the food superb. Somewhere the Great Minds had found a string quartet, which provided enchanting background music. All in all, everything was "just right."

Hollister took care to introduce Amy to all three of the Great Minds, and noted that they took the time and effort to make her feel completely at ease and welcome. Most of the conversation, of course, was typical holiday party chitchat.

Every now and then Hollister noted that a couple would slip into one office or another, close the door, and not be seen for a half-hour or so. He knew that if he were alone he'd be tracking down some of that alluring "strange stuff," which seemed to be present in abundance. Since he and Amy were together, and on their best behavior, nothing like that happened. When they got back to Hollister's room, though, the party spirit lingered and their lovemaking was fantastic!

THE NEXT WORLD

The rest of their time together was wonderfully relaxed, and all too short, as both Art and Amy had known it would be. The Midwinter Holiday party at Unit 414 was, of course, delightful—but sort of an anti-climax for Art and Amy after the bash at Main Administration the previous Friday. Since this was Amy's last night with Art until their scheduled get together the following summer, they left the party rather early, and spent the rest of the evening in the most appropriate way they could think of.

The Frolicsome Four postponed their monthly get together for one day, and shortly after noon on Sunday the 31st they began partying. When the time came, they adjourned to the great room on the top floor for the First Annual Building KK 280 New Year's Eve Party.

Everything was absolutely first class, including the entertainment. On this occasion, working on a raised platform so that everyone could see, Nina Stivers entertained the crowd with an incredible strip tease lasting 15 minutes. The dance itself, and the music accompanying it, would have done proud any burlesque house on Earth. The crowd's response was a roaring, cheering, whistling standing ovation!

It was almost a letdown when, the next afternoon, Farnsworth, Wilkinson and Hollister drank beer and listened to a radio description of a lackluster Rose Bowl game, in which Columbia defeated Stanford 7–0.

Chapter 16

1993

On October 6th in the year 1993, Arthur Hollister, deep in reverie, observed the 60th anniversary of his own death. An awful lot had happened on Earth and in The Next World, and some very important things remained to be done.

The United States had been involved in 3 major wars during the previous 60 years, and several minor campaigns. The country had lost two presidents by death in office, one due to natural causes and one by assassination. A third president, disgraced and in the shadow of impeachment, had resigned.

One of America's main problems at the moment was rampant crime, much of it related to trafficking in illegal narcotics. A series of weak presidential administrations, coupled with greedy, corrupt congresses, had tried to be all things to all people, and had lost all concept of fiscal responsibility. The national debt had become astronomical, yet the gutless wonders running the country couldn't even balance the national budget, much less begin paying off the debt.

The collusion between medical care providers, pharmaceutical houses, insurance companies and the legal profession dominated the entire health care

THE NEXT WORLD

scene. The feeble efforts by various politicians, most of them lawyers by trade, to "reform" the health care situation were a pathetic joke.

Substantial portions of the American population seemed content to feed at the public trough, and were ready to blame everyone but themselves for their problems.

Certain individuals, such as professional athletes, movie stars and others in the entertainment industry were grossly overpaid. As long as the public remained gullible enough to pay to watch them, that situation would continue.

Fortunately, most of those who were willing to work for a living seemed to be "getting by," while others were living quite comfortably.

On the international scene, countries or portions of their populations were still trying to settle their differences by killing each other. Many of the underlying problems involved religious differences. In other cases the problems were rooted in racial strife, or the eternal struggle between the "haves" and the "have nots." A lot of the time, it appeared, as it has throughout human history, that what the "have nots" lacked was brain power or even common sense.

The major problems facing the Earth were dreadful over-population, and the pollution and depletion of natural resources that such human proliferation engenders. Religious beliefs and outright human stupidity seemed to have gone hand in hand to cause the population problems, aided by various efforts to provide food and medical care to those who otherwise might not have survived.

Already, natural controls is the form of pestilence, specifically the epidemic spread of the AIDS virus, were decimating the human population. Inevitably, other problems of a far more monstrous and overwhelming sort would eventually plague the human populace, unless its numbers were somehow controlled.

On a lighter note, the college football scene in the U.S. had been a pleasure to follow, first by radio, and brief written accounts shown on the television screen, then by black & white television, and now by high quality color television transmissions. Some of the highlights which had been particularly noteworthy to Hollister, Wilkinson and Farnsworth included:

The 1934 season, when Michigan came in dead last in the Big Ten.

The 1942 season, in which Wisconsin came in second in the Big Ten, but defeated eventual National Champion Ohio State 17-7 in the process.

The 1948 Northwestern team's 20-14 victory over California in the 1949 Rose Bowl.

The 1952, 1959 and 1962 Wisconsin Teams, all of which won or tied for the Big Ten Championship, then lost in the Rose Bowl.

The 23 times during that 60 year stretch when Michigan won or tied for the Big Ten Championship.

As televised sports coverage had gotten better, the trio had enjoyed numerous pro football games, the Olympic games, a number of college basketball games, lots of professional golf tournaments and a few other events, but their first love had remained Big Ten football.

On the TNW scene, there had also been some changes. As of January 1, 1942, the Great Minds modified two major facets of recycling. First, souls of newly deceased individuals were required to recycle immediately unless they had already served three or more lifetimes on Earth. Those souls who had served three lifetimes or more were, as before, given the option to recycle or to remain in TNW.

All souls residing in TNW as of January 1, 1942, who had not yet served three or more "tours of duty" on Earth, were urged to recycle promptly, but were not forced to do so.

Finally, as of that same date, all souls who recycled—both the freshly dead and those who had resided in TNW for years before recycling—were given their choices of skin color, gender, sexual orientation, and country of birth. They were guaranteed good general health, but not necessarily long or happy lives. If disease, accident, foul play or act of war befell them, so be it. Even if a soul's time on Earth proved to be very short, it would still count as a "lifetime" in TNW records.

Over the years, Hollister received a number of suggestions and comments from TNW residents. The vast majority of these residents were content to stay in TNW forever, and many volunteered to help out in one way or another, and thus make themselves useful. Different floors in different buildings organized classes in all sorts of things.

Souls who had been teachers in their previous lives frequently offered to give televised lecture series on subjects such as History, Art, Literature, English, Music and the like. Many such telecasts were made available to TNW residents, and most of them proved very popular.

As all of TNW experienced population changes, so did Unit 414. Of the original 16 residents, 4 recycled during the first 60 years. Eleanor Atkinson, the young lady who had died in an auto crash at age 17, left in 1937. Fred Feingold, the former Munich Jeweler, and Henry Petz, the former telephone man from Cincinnati, both left in January of 1942, soon after the new policies on recycling were announced. Rod Mitchell, who had been a 20-year-old Assistant Store Manager at the time of his death, hung around until 1955.

The other 12 original members of the Unit 414 aggregation, each one of whom had 3 or more previous lifetimes to his or her credit, remained happily residing there 60 years later. None looked a day older than in 1933!

Hollister had become thoroughly familiar with the TNW set-up, had visited most of the restaurants and recreational facilities, and had played hundreds of TNW's golf courses, usually playing in a foursome with the Great Minds.

Over the years, Hollister had repeatedly explored the four Headquarters Buildings, and had become well acquainted with the staffs in all of them. TNW was almost 100 years old, yet every building was operating to perfection! Main Administration was 40% empty, and was expected to stay pretty much that way for centuries to come. There was no need for empire building in TNW, and those who proposed it were gently but effectively dissuaded.

Hollister still watched in wonderment as Enhanced Production, with the setting of a few dials and the pushing of a couple of buttons, created a thousand or more housing units at a crack, out of nothing. In another department, foodstuffs were cranked out at an incredible pace, while furnishings, equipment, supplies and all other components of the good life in TNW were turned out as needed in other areas of the building.

Enhanced Production worked hand-in-hand with Central Supply, which managed distribution of everything to where it was needed. Enhanced Production periodically

THE NEXT WORLD 119

dispatched couriers to Earth to bring back samples of new items to be reproduced in TNW, and subsequently distributed for the benefit of occupants.

Enhanced Production could also send a TNW resident back to Earth on any sort of properly-authorized special mission. So far Hollister had not made a return trip to Earth, but he expected to make one in the very near future.

At this precise moment, however, Hollister was feeling rather depressed. He'd just learned the official death totals for Planet Earth for the year 1992. The figure exceeded 495,000,000 people. Even with the many souls who recycled at once, that filled an awful lot of space in TNW, and the outlook for 1993 and future years was even more grim, particularly because Earth's birth rate was outstripping its huge death rate.

It was, Hollister realized, time for a serious meeting with Sam Schwartz, Olga Olson and Harry Hendricks. Hollister picked up his phone, made a call, and arranged to meet with the Great Minds the next day, Thursday, October 7, 1993, at 9:00 a.m.

Chapter 17

After greeting the Great Minds, Hollister got right down to business. "My friends," Hollister began, "something is really bothering me. Our birthplace, dear old Planet Earth, is dreadfully overpopulated, and the situation is getting worse year after year. Only a relatively small portion of the world's population has shown the common sense and foresight to employ voluntary methods of birth control.

The Biblical 'Go Forth and Multiply' obsession, promulgated for centuries by the Catholic Church and other misguided Christian groups, has been a major cause of the present problem, but far from the only one.

"To my knowledge, only one major country, China, has adopted a vigorous national population policy, their one child per couple program. Even at that, their national population, already the largest of any nation on Earth, continues to grow.

"In general, mankind knows that as population on Earth grows, the quality of life there diminishes. Those with any brains realize that unless human population is curtailed, drastic consequences will follow sooner or later. One classic contributor to population control, War, is presently pretty much out of fashion. Two others, Pestilence and Famine, are waiting in the wings licking their ghoulish chops. When one or both of those two really strike the human populace, they'll probably give their old buddy War a boost in the process. One gruesome way or another the world's population will ultimately diminish, but by then who knows whether the world be fit to live in.

"So, with mankind basically unwilling and unable to save itself, thereby dooming the planet the human race inhabits, I'd say man needs some outside help."

"It's hard to refute fact and logic, Art," replied Sam Schwartz, as Olga Olson and Harry Hendricks nodded in agreement.

"As you know, however, we here in TNW have never really meddled with Earth's goings on. We've watched what was happening, sometimes applauding and often condemning, but that's been about it. We've sent our messengers to Earth to pick up samples of things we could reproduce here in TNW, and distribute for the entertainment, amusement, amazement, comfort or education of the TNW populace, but that's been just about our only contact with live Earthlings. Just exactly what is it you have in mind, Art?"

"I think the answer may lie in the Wonderful Central Processor. Suppose that a percentage of souls being sent to Earth, both the recycled ones and the newly-created ones, were modified so that the new bodies they were born into would be sterile. The people so affected would appear normal in every way, but when they reached reproductive age they would simply be unable to have children. What do you three think of the idea so far?"

"What you're suggesting," said Harry Hendricks, "is that we play God. I have some misgivings about your proposal, but I'll reserve my decision until later."

"How would you decide who got sterile souls and who got fertile ones?" Olga Olson inquired.

"Do you propose," asked Sam Schwartz, "a straight, across the board, distribution of sterile souls on a random basis, or would you favor certain races or nationalities with a higher percentage of fertile souls, and penalize others by infusing their populations with a larger number of sterile souls?"

"There you've reached the crux of the matter, Sam, and I don't pretend to have a positive answer. We could be entirely 'fair' about it, determine a starting percentage of sterile souls, and apply it to the world's entire population. Or, with the help of a committee who were population experts on Earth, we could establish a system of priorities. Such an approach would reward those portions of the World's populace which had shown the sense to limit their reproduction rates with higher fertility, and penalize those groups who tended to thoughtlessly breed like rabbits by rendering a higher percentage of them sterile.

"We have to bear in mind," Hollister continued, "that anything we do will take more than a generation to affect Earth's population at all. By the year 2020, there will be close to 8 billion people on Earth according to latest projections. This mass of humanity will be draining the world's resources at an incredible rate, and reducing the quality of human life dreadfully.

"What we don't know is whether widespread famine or pestilence will have set in to help balance things out. My gut feeling is that we have to step into the picture now. Given my druthers, I'd set a goal of reducing the Earth's population to about two billion by the year 2100. I'd definitely institute a priority system, ensuring that eventually a high proportion of the world's population would be intelligent, productive and responsible in its outlook. If that meant we were practicing human eugenics, so be it. In my opinion, adopting a program such as I've described would be one of the greatest gifts we could give to mankind!"

Harry Hendricks broke in at this point. "Art, I have to admit that your points are extremely well taken. I still have a few misgivings about meddling into the lives of humankind, but at this juncture I suspect that unless we act, the situation will soon be beyond salvage."

"I agree with Harry," Olga Olson said. "Art's idea about creating an advisory committee of population experts is a good one, but I think there are a few things we should establish at the outset. First, we are setting a definite goal to reduce Earth's population to about 2 billion people by the year 2100. Second, we will monitor the situation over the years, prepared to make adjustments if necessary. Third, we'll select our committee members carefully, make sure they represent a good cross section of the world's racial make-up, and hold the group's size down to, say, five. If they work together well, great. If not, we'll make replacements until we get a group that does."

"A few other points we have to consider," Sam Schwartz added. "I think our emphasis should be on sterilizing females in whatever percentages are finally agreed up on. It is the only approach that makes sense, until or unless men start having babies.

"We have to face potential repercussions here in TNW. With Earth's population diminishing because of our program, we will have a much smaller demand for recycled souls, and probably no need for newly-created souls. I forsee such things as waiting lists for souls who wish to recycle, an end to mandatory multiple recycling, institution of higher quality standards for retention of souls of the freshly dead, and so on. We may have to begin processing more souls of basic human garbage into nothingness. These would include almost everyone in the drug trade, most murderers and other serious criminals whose exploits on Earth we have tended to overlook in the past.

We could also offer souls in TNW who are so bored with afterlife that they don't want to continue with it anymore the opportunity to be processed into nothingness. Others might simply opt to be put into long-term storage for 50 years, 100 years, 500 years or more—whatever they chose.

Even with all the things I have just mentioned, we'll have to face the probability that we will have to vastly expand TNW's facilities. That's the basic price we'll have to pay for our efforts to save deal old Mother Earth.

Also, I think we should work quietly on this. The director of Central Processing should probably sit in with the advisory committee. We four will have to give final approval, of course, before the program is initiated.

"Okay," Schwartz continued, "everybody in favor of this program to preserve the Earth by reducing its human population say Aye."

By a unanimous vote, the Great Minds approved the idea, and Schwartz promised to contact Central Processing, and obtain the names of a dozen candidates for the TNW Population of Earth Advisory Committee. Schwartz then asked Hollister if he had anything else to put before the group.

"As a matter of fact, I do," Hollister replied. "I'm awfully glad you went along with my human population control proposal, since it makes me feel a lot better about my second project. And, by the way, if I'm not present to vote on the actual implementation of the population project, please register my vote as you feel I myself would have.

"Now, I'm going to let you in on something I've been keeping secret. For the past two years I've been writing a book. Entitled *Fear Not The Future*, my book is intended for publication and distribution on Earth. This book will tell everyone on Earth, who reads it or hears about it, the story of The Next World. For the first time, the public will learn about the very pleasant future life that awaits the vast majority of people after they die. This may get some of the folks in the 'God Business' upset, but it should put the minds of millions of people at rest.

"I intend to take my manuscript back to Earth, and arrange to have it published. There may be promotional work I have to do as well, so I'll need what I believe the airlines call an open return trip reservation. I could possibly be on Earth for up to a year before returning to TNW. Once I finish the book publication business, I'll be ready to settle down for a good long stretch of R&R here in TNW. Hopefully, we'll be watching the success of our Population of Earth project during the next century or so.

"Now, assuming the three of you have no objection to my book project, or to my proposed visit to Earth, I'd appreciate your telling me all of the ins and outs of making such a trip. I've nosed into just about everything else here in TNW, but regarding a journey of this type, all I know is that it's possible. I'm vague on the details."

Sam, Harry and Olga quickly agreed to Hollister's book idea. Schwartz then began to tell Hollister some of the details of travel back to Earth.

"Back in the very beginning, the Baldonians helped us set up a system for sending souls back to Earth on special errands. All traveling souls leave from a special section in Enhanced Production, and go to a facility in upstate New York, which is owned and operated by Volunteer Efforts Agency. The Agency earns no income, pays no salaries and pays no taxes.

"By, shall we say, very special arrangements with a nearby small town bank, deposits of funds are periodically credited to a secret VEA account. That same bank handles payment of all bills incurred by VEA, including credit card balances as they become due, and disburses such cash amounts as are required by VEA or visiting TNW residents. When I'm done with my part of this story, I'll let Harry tell you the fascinating story of where those special funds come from.

"Volunteer Efforts Agency is entirely staffed by souls from TNW who rotate in, work there for a few months, and then return to TNW. The staff, which always numbers seven people, has very little to do, but always handles its duties expertly.

"When those on errands from TNW arrive, VEA provides them with money, credit cards, clothing and so on. The staff also helps the visitors make travel arrangements, and handles the details of shipping items purchased by visitors back to TNW.

"When Olga, Harry and I made a trip back to Earth in 1939, to take care of some TNW business and to visit the New York World's Fair, the VEA staff took excellent care of us, although none of them realized that we were the bosses here in TNW.

"Those who travel back to Earth are mortal while there, and just as vulnerable to accident, illness or foul play as any human. They eat regular food, evacuate wastes just as any human does, and if they drink enough booze they become drunk and wake up with a hangover. The only difference between our temporarily mortal TNW visitors to Earth and other humans is that all the folks from TNW are sterile.

"Should someone from TNW die while on Earth, he ends up here in TNW again, and is processed right back to his old rooming unit. In the roughly 94 years TNW has been operating, we've had 7 TNW visitors to Earth die in auto accidents, two die in airplane crashes, and one each succumb to food poisoning, typhoid fever, heart attack and murder. All of those folks were back as souls in TNW within a couple of days.

"Our toughest problem came when one of our guys was thrown in jail on a trumped-up charge. We finally had to enlist the help of one of our souls who had been a great criminal lawyer in his time. He went back to Earth, found the town where our guy was being held, dazzled the local authorities with footwork and secured our guy's release. In other words, we take care of our own.

"You can be sure, Art, that if you get in trouble on Earth we'll make every effort to rescue you. Nonetheless, take care. Now, Harry, tell Art where all the money comes from, the cash that keeps our Earthly bank account well-filled."

"As Sam has hinted, Art, it's an interesting story. Every year thousands of people die, having left behind small, and large, fortunes in cash and other valuables, hidden so well that in most cases no one would ever find them. When the Wonderful Central Processor encounters the soul of such an individual, his record is flagged for special interviewing.

"Sometimes a soul begs us to let his needy, or greedy, relatives know where the money is hidden. Often, however, the soul is happy to tell us where the money is, so that we can retrieve it for the good of all the souls here in TNW. On certain occasions we actually mail anonymous letters on Earth, to let heirs know where the cash is stashed. In other instances, we send TNW people on treasure hunts all over the world, and their finds have been truly amazing!

"It's those funds which have allowed us to buy the latest in electronics, furniture, clothing and all kinds of other neat stuff on Earth, for reproduction here in TNW, and distribution to our residents. In the early days we sometimes sent TNW agents into the future to make purchases. Now, though, we're content to obtain new items each year as they come on the market."

"And now, Art," Olga asked, do you have someone in mind to take your place in our golf foursome while you're off adventuring?"

"Yes, Olga, I do. I've sort of kept her hidden away from you folks all these years in case you ever asked me to come up with a partner in a mixed doubles match. However, I've already asked the lady, name of Roberta Jones, whether she'd be willing to fill in for me while I'm gone. Bobbie has agreed, and all you have to do is call her to set up your first golf date. She lives in Room 15, in the same rooming unit as I do. My only worry is that once you've played golf with Bobbie, you won't want to go back to having me in your foursome!"

"No fear of that, Art, said Olga. "You, I can beat once in a while. Your friend Bobbie may prove to be a ringer, and clean all of our clocks! Now go ahead, have a safe trip, and wow us with stories of your travels when you get back."

After that, no one found much to say. Hollister shook hands with Schwartz and Hendricks, gave Olga a big hug, and left the Great Minds' office. It would be a long time before he saw any of them again.

Chapter 18

Before leaving the area, Hollister stopped at Enhanced Production, went to the Travel Section, and made arrangements for a journey to Earth the following Monday morning. When asked if he would be carrying anything with him, Hollister replied that he would be taking one 3 1/2" computer floppy disk. The Travel Section Chief supplied Hollister with a special, pocket-sized envelope which would protect the disk and Hollister's All Purpose Card during the trip. The gentleman also explained that, on the day of his departure, Hollister should expect about 15 minutes of special processing before his trip began. Unlike airline travel, there was no specified hour of departure. When Hollister was ready to go, Travel Section would accommodate him.

That night at dinner, Hollister found himself sitting with a group that included all the souls who had replaced others from Unit 414 who had recycled. Charles Eagan, a former mail carrier from Ft. Lauderdale, had replaced Rodney Mitchell in 1955. Richard Collins, a former Airline Pilot, had replaced Fred Feingold in 1942, the same year that Adolph Hoffmeister, a former lawyer, had replaced Henry Petz. Colleen Flannigan, a charming redhead, had replaced Eleanor Atkinson way back in 1937, which made her the old timer among the newcomers. Colleen had been a champion tennis player in her time, and had been delighted that she could pursue her interest in the sport in TNW. Colleen had been giving tennis lessons to TNW residents for years, and thoroughly enjoying herself in the process.

After dinner, Hollister sought out the other members of the Frolicsome Four, urging them to break any plans they might have had for the following Saturday and attend a get together in Hollister's room that afternoon, with said little gathering very likely to continue well into the evening. Since Wilkinson and Hollister would have gotten together to watch football that afternoon anyway, it was up to Thelma and Alma, and both charming ladies readily agreed to join the gentlemen on Saturday, October 9, 1993. Hollister tantalized the others a bit, promising them all some very special news.

On Friday, Hollister made final preparations for his trip to Earth. From the hard drive on his computer he made 3 copies of his book manuscript on separate 3 1/2" discs. He decided to take two disks with him, and to leave the third copy with Bryce Wilkinson for safe-keeping.

Hollister knew that making any detailed plans for his trip at this point would be a waste of time and energy. He knew the primary mission of his trip to Earth, and that he would start out by looking up one particular man, who at this point in time would be about 47 years old. Hollister had made a search of Central Processing's records, and made sure that the man he sought had never been processed into TNW, although dozens of others with the same name had been. He was sure that David Curtis was still alive, and somewhere on Earth Hollister would find him!

That evening, Hollister put through a telephone call to Amy Lawrence. He told her about his forthcoming trip to Earth, shared with her the exciting news about the book he had written, and explained that the duration of his stay on Earth was uncertain. Hollister promised Amy that he'd get back in touch with her as soon as he returned to TNW, and asked her not to worry about him in the meantime. Wanting to be honest about the situation, Hollister said that his absence could last a year or more, that their semi-annual visits with each other would have to be put on hold until he got back, and that he'd see Amy as soon as he could after his return to TNW.

On Saturday morning, Hollister made lavish preparations for what he knew would be the last gathering of the Frolicsome Four for many months to come. They hadn't missed a monthly get together in 60 years, and he hated to be the one to break the string. After arranging for a wide variety of snacks and drinks for the afternoon, Hollister made dinner reservations for four at one of the group's favorite restaurants. As a final touch, he arranged for building supply to provide three extra easy chairs and a coffee table. They'd be watching the game in comfort that afternoon!
In what seemed to be no time, Hollister's guests arrived and everyone settled in for some serious football viewing. Watching live football telecasts, in color on a 27" screen, was a far cry from the early days when all they'd had available were play-by-play radio accounts.
This game was a special one. The Northwestern Wildcats, who had spoiled Wisconsin's hopes for a bowl game the season before, were guests at Wisconsin's 1993 Homecoming, and the Badgers were out for blood! The unbeaten Badgers got their revenge that day, whipping the Wildcats 53 to 14. Bryce Wilkinson was in a state of Euphoria, and with a start Hollister realized that back on Earth, David Curtis was undoubtedly feeling the same way, and had probably attended the game in person.

As the game ended, the Frolicsome Four would normally have been shedding their clothes as rapidly as they could, in anticipation of some delightful fun in the sack. This time, however, Hollister asked the others to hold off on that a bit, as he had something to tell them. Having gained their attention, he told Thelma, Alma and Bryce about the book he had written, the trip he would be making to Earth with a view to having the book published, and that he'd be gone for a number of months, perhaps for a year or more.

"And so, my dear friends," Hollister continued, "I'll be with you in spirit on the last Saturday of each month, but it's likely to be some time before I'll be back with you in fact. I hope you continue to get together as a trio, rather than bringing some other guy into the act, but if you two are more than a Wisconsin man can handle, well—."

"Your spot in our group is secure Art, and we'll be thinking of you, wishing you well and awaiting your return," said Alma.

"What Alma said goes double for me," Thelma added.

"We'll miss you, old buddy," said Wilkinson. "And don't worry, my friend, this old Wisconsin alum can take care of these ladies the way the Badgers are taking care of the opposition this fall. In case you haven't noticed, my alma mater is 5-0 so far these season. I really think this is the year for you to cheer for the Cardinal and White—if you want to be backing a winner, that is!

"On a serious note, Art, if there's any way the three of us can help you with this project, either here in TNW or back on Earth, please be sure to let us know!"

From then on, taking only the break to go out to dinner, the Frolicsome Four lived up to their name.

Chapter 19

After Sunday dinner the next day, Hollister stood up, asked for the group's attention, and told the other 15 residents of Unit 414 that he'd be leaving them for a while, on an extended business trip to Earth.

The following morning, as he left his room and headed toward the elevator, Hollister was surprised and delighted to see all the others from his unit lining the hallway, waiting to shake his hand or give him a hug as they wished him well and said that they'd miss him. Fittingly, the last three awaiting him were Alma, Thelma and Bryce. Hollister embraced them all, kissed each lady, and grasped Wilkinson's hand warmly one last time, before he left Unit 414 and proceeded out of the building and on to Enhanced Production.

Charles Smith, the Travel Section Chief, was waiting for Hollister, who was to be his only "customer" that day.

"Good morning, Mr. Hollister. All set for your first visit to Earth since 1933?"

"Good morning, Mr. Smith," Hollister replied. "I'm as ready to travel as I'll ever be, and I have to admit I'm looking forward to the trip. Since I've watched all manner of movies, TV shows, newscasts and the like over the years, I won't be as surprised by what it's like on Earth now as I would have if I'd simply been doing a triple *Rip Van Winkle,* and sleeping the last 60 years. Nonetheless, I expect the experience to be fascinating. Now, what's the next step?"

Inviting Hollister to have a seat near his desk, Smith asked Hollister the purpose of his trip, the anticipated duration, and what he'd be taking with him. Hollister replied that the trip would be mainly business, he'd be gone for between 6 and 18 months, and he was taking two 3 1/2" floppy computer discs with him, plus, of course, his All Purpose Card.

"And now, Mr. Hollister, a couple of additional things. Do you want to appear essentially as you do now while on Earth, or would you rather appear older or perhaps younger? And, do you have any particular questions at this time?"

"I'm used to how I look now, and content with my present appearance. I do, as you might expect, have some questions. First, how long does the trip to Earth take, and will I be conscious during that trip? Second, at what point do I become mortal? Third, are there any particular precautions I should take?"

"The trip covers a great distance, and actually takes six hours. You'll be in a state of suspended animation, however, and it will seem to you that you get there as fast as you travel from one point to another here in TNW. You become mortal when you safely reach the sending and receiving chamber at the Volunteer Efforts Agency in upstate New York. The VEA staff will supply you with anything you need, answer any further questions you have, and help you get oriented as an Earthling again.

"With your computer discs and All Purpose Card safely in their protective pouch, and that pouch tucked into one of your inside suit coat pockets, you're all set to go. Please step through that door, into the sending and receiving chamber, and take a seat. The chamber is rather large, as you'll see, because we receive some sizeable inbound shipments from time to time."

After thanking the Travel Chief, Hollister stepped into the chamber, then seated himself in a comfortable chair. At this point, the door to the chamber closed. Hollister leaned back to relax, shut his eyes for a moment, and then became aware that the door to the chamber had opened again. Expecting to see Smith appear to check on some last minute detail, Hollister was surprised to see an attractive lady, dressed in a bright orange jump suit. At about the same moment, Hollister had a sensation he hadn't felt in over 60 years. He really needed to urinate!

"Good afternoon, sir, and welcome to Earth," said the lady.

"Good afternoon, ma'am," said Hollister. "Could you please direct me to the, er, sanitary facilities?"

"Out this door and right across the hall, sir. Seems like everyone who comes in from TNW has to pee, before they can concentrate on anything else. I know I do, every time I return to Earth."

A few minutes later, feeling much relieved, Hollister once again approached the lady who had greeted him. Presenting his All Purpose Card, he waited until the lady had scanned it.

"Well, Mr. Hollister," the lady exclaimed, "you have the highest priority level there is! It means that whatever you want, you can have, and wherever you want to go, you can. I, by the way, am Annabelle Thompkins."

Hollister took another look at the lady, and realized that she was a real knockout. A voluptuous strawberry blonde in her early 20's, Annabelle Thompkins stood about 5 foot 8, had spectacular big green eyes and a smile that could set any man's hormones stirring!. With a start, Hollister realized that his was a mortal, human, body for the first time in six decades, and that indeed the sight of Annabelle Thompkins, and the aroma of the delightful scent she was wearing, had set his heart pounding and his blood racing!

Finally, Hollister spoke. "Right now, Annabelle, the thing I want to do more than anything is to make love to you. I haven't done such a thing as a mortal for over 60 years, and I find you so overwhelmingly attractive that I can't get myself focused on anything else."

    Annabelle glanced up at the clock, which read 2:55. Turning to Art, she said "My relief gets here in 5 minutes. When he does, we can go to my cottage just down the road, and I'll try to give *you* some relief. Not because of your high status in TNW, you understand, but because right now I'm feeling just as horny as you are!

    Two hours later, wearing only a pair of slippers and a frilly apron, Annabelle began preparing Hollister the first meal of real food he'd had in sixty years. On the menu were a thick, juicy sirloin steak, baked stuffed potatoes, gourmet quality canned early June peas, fresh fruit salad, hot flaky dinner rolls and, for dessert, warm pecan pie a la mode.

    Hollister watched her for a while, then ambled into the living room, where he sat in a comfortable recliner chair, completely bemused. He had just made love three times in two hours, more sex than he'd enjoyed in that short a time span, on Earth, since he was a randy young 19-year-old just learning what sex was all about! What's more, Hollister knew that if he'd stayed in the kitchen watching Annabelle bounce around in that skimpy apron for another five minutes, he'd become aroused again!

    Although his original intent had been to get on immediately with efforts to get his book published and promoted, Hollister knew that a few weeks delay wouldn't matter all that much. They'd told him he could have whatever he asked for while he was on Earth, and right now Hollister had a pretty good idea what he wanted. He'd go over it all with Annabelle tomorrow, when he officially processed in for his visit to Earth. At the moment, Hollister looked forward to enjoying a great meal, and after that to more of the greatest sex he'd ever had!

As his official in-processing proceeded the next morning, Annabelle asked Hollister what special requirements he had.

"Well," replied Hollister, "Let's see. I'll need a couple of major credit cards, each with no less than a $100,000 limit. I need some walking around money, too, say $100,000 in cash, and a phone number to call whenever I need to replenish my cash supply.

"Then, to be on the safe side, I'll need a U.S. Passport, a New York drivers license and a Social Security card. You can use yesterday's date, in the year 1966, as my date of birth. I don't think anyone would believe I was born in 1875! For transportation, I plan to buy a new car, which is to be registered to Volunteer Efforts Agency and insured by VEA. One of the credit cards you supply me with should be in the name of the VEA, showing me as an authorized signatory. I'll select the car and the auto insurance I want, and charge them to the VEA credit card.

"Most of all, Annabelle, I'd like to have you as my sometime chauffeur and full-time traveling companion. My stay on Earth could be as short as 6 months, or as long as 18 months, and while I'm here I want you with me. So, if you're willing to accompany me, please make the necessary arrangements with TNW, and also supply yourself with a passport, credit cards and other appropriate documents.

"Please arrange for the two of us to have all the various inoculations that a prudent U.S. citizen of this day and age would have, plus any special ones we might require for travel to Europe, Scandinavia, or the Orient, particularly China, Hong Kong and Japan. To become immunized against certain diseases, we will each need a series of shots. So, please obtain certified shot records for each of us to carry, plus whatever additional documents we'll need to convince physicians or clinics to provide us with further shots. Oh, yes, one more thing. Please arrange for top quality, no limit, medical and hospital insurance for both of us. Our identification cards should, once again, show that we are employed by the Volunteer Efforts Agency. So, do you want to come with me or what?"

"How does that old saying go, Art? Wild horses couldn't keep me away. Tours here at VEA are usually limited to about two month's duration, during which we aren't supposed to wander more that about 50 miles from VEA headquarters. It sounds as if you'll be going lots of places, meeting interesting people and doing exciting things. If you want me with you, I'll be delighted to accompany you. And besides, you're an awfully good lay!"

"Thanks for the compliment, sweetheart. I'm both delighted and incredibly relieved that you'll be traveling with me. You and I haven't known each other very long, but I already feel that had I met you during the early days of my last lifetime, say about the turn of the century, I'd have latched onto you and never let go! In fact, if you had been willing, I'd have married you—and that's something Arthur Hollister has never said to a woman before, in this world or the next!"

"Someday, Art, I'll tell you how old I was in 1900. For that matter, I assume that as we travel around, by automobile, airplane or whatever, we'll tell each other our entire stories, about our lives on Earth and our years in TNW."

"Annabelle, if I didn't know that you'd already been working your present tour on Earth for about a month, I'd think you were a special gift to me from my close friends, the Great Minds of The Next World. I look forward to the time we'll be together, as I've never looked forward to anything else. Now, how long before we can begin our travels?"

"I'll arrange an appointment for the two of us to get our inoculations tomorrow at the Elmwood Clinic. In the meantime, today we'll stop past the documents section with a list of our requirements. They'll shoot our passport photos, and get cranking on everything we need. I'll notify TNW that I'm required on an extended assignment with you, and that they should send out a replacement for me right away.

"Tomorrow in Elmwood, that's a small town about 15 miles away, you can pick up a few clothes and other items to tide you over. You can simply draw a few hundred dollars from our petty cash fund to cover that. We should be ready to begin our travels on Thursday morning, and I'll arrange for your special currency delivery to take place about 9:00 a.m. that day. By the way, where will we be going?"

"Let's start out by heading for Utica. We'll take care of some business there, and play things by ear after that. Can you arrange for one of the other staff members to drive us to Utica on Thursday, leaving here about ten?"

"No problem, Art. And, by the way, am I correct in assuming that you'll be staying with me tonight and tomorrow night?"

"Only if you ask me to."

"Consider yourself invited. Is there anything else you need arranged?"

"Only one matter I can think of, Annabelle. Can you, or someone else on the staff, give me a short refresher course on driving? The last car I drove was a 1933 Cadillac, and that was in 1933. I need to become familiar with modern cars, highways, driving conditions and traffic laws."

"I'm a pretty good driver, Art, but we've had other requests like yours over the years, and have made special arrangements with the Acme Driving School in Esterbrook. I'll call them, and I'm sure they'll be able to get an expert teacher over here, with a car, right after lunch today. My guess is that by the end of the afternoon you'll feel really refreshed in the driving department. After all, driving a car is one thing you never really forget how to do, just like riding a bicycle or making love. Now, let's get over to the document section and get them started on what we need."

Chapter 20

Hollister, Annabelle and their driver stopped for lunch at a fast food place on the outskirts of Utica. Hollister found the food less than spectacular. Somehow he longed for the greasy cheeseburgers and fries he remembered from long ago. They'd had a flavor and character that seemed totally lacking in the production line stuff they were eating now. Nonetheless, the food sated their hunger, and the place did have clean rest rooms.

After lunch, Art and Annabelle found their way to what seemed to be the city's leading Chrysler dealership. They parked, and while the driver settled down to peruse the newspaper he'd purchased from a rack outside the restaurant, Art and Annabelle entered the new car showroom and shopped for an automobile. When it came time to take a test drive, Hollister's refresher driving course from two days earlier stood him in good stead. He knew he had just the car he needed when he selected a shiny black 1994 Chrysler LHS 4-door sedan. The automobile was roomy, well-appointed, and a real pleasure to drive. The 18 cubic feet of trunk space was icing on the cake.

Hollister told the salesman to write up the deal, which came to roughly $33,000 including sales tax and registration fees. When Hollister proffered a credit card as payment in full, the salesman seemed a bit surprised and excused himself, saying that he had to consult with his sales manager. The salesman returned a few minutes later, smiling broadly. He had obviously checked, and found that the credit card was good as gold.

"And now," said Hollister, "I'm going to throw a little garbage in the game. Before I sign that sales contract, I want you to add two provisions. One is that I take delivery at this time tomorrow, the second is that you have the car fully registered, and the new license plates on it, when I pick it up. I count on you to take care of the registration matter personally, even if you have to drive to Albany this afternoon, register the car first thing in the morning and then drive right back with the plates and papers. I think you'll want to do this for me, in fact I can think off hand of a thousand dancing green reasons why you should.

"There's just one more thing. I like the cut of that suit you're wearing—it shows you have good taste in clothing. So, after I've signed the sales agreement and you've provided me with my copy, I'd like you to step outside and tell our driver how to get to a good men's clothing store, possibly in a large shopping mall where all manner of items are available, including fine women's clothing, too."

"No problem on any of those things, Mr. Hollister. I'll see that the car is prepped, registered and ready to go by 3:00 tomorrow afternoon. There's a great shopping mall, called Rosewood Center, just a couple of miles from here, and I'll be happy to tell your driver how to get there. Now, if you'll just sign here, I'll give you a copy of the contract and you'll be all set."

Rosewood Center seemed to have just about everything, including a bank, a general insurance agency, a large food court and all manner of stores, both large and small. Hollister gave the driver $500 and told him to buy himself something, then go back and wait for them in the car. He then aimed Annabelle at a ladies' wear shop, telling her to buy whatever she wanted and then wait for him. Once Annabelle was happily occupied, Hollister went to the insurance agency, had them bind coverage on the new Chrysler, and paid them a full year's premium on the spot. The agent supplied Hollister with temporary insurance ID cards, and agreed to have the policy and permanent ID cards mailed to Hollister, in care of Volunteer Efforts Agency.

During the next couple of hours, on his own, Hollister shopped primarily for clothing items which might have to be altered. A well-stocked men's store had some excellent all weather suits, the coats of which fitted Hollister's 6 foot 3 inch frame perfectly. When the salesman promised that any necessary alterations could be completed by noon the following day, Hollister bought three suits, a couple of sports coats, several pairs of slacks and a weatherproof topcoat with a zip-in liner.

Annabelle, meanwhile, bought an assortment of coordinated garments, suitable for mix and match or wear as separates. On one of the luckiest shopping days of her life, everything she liked fitted her perfectly. She was on a roll, and had herself a ball! Even the raincoat she selected required no alterations. Like Hollister, Annabelle deferred purchase of more mundane items until the next day, when she would also be picking up the garments she was selecting now.

When they met at a pre-selected spot two hours later, neither Art nor Annabelle was carrying a single package. They returned to the VEA car, and asked the driver, who was now sporting a blue and silver Detroit Lions jacket, with cap to match, to take them to a motel they had seen earlier. Before leaving the car to go in and register, Hollister asked the driver if he would like a room for the night, too. The driver declined, saying he'd just as soon head back to his own cottage at VEA once Hollister and Annabelle were all set. A few minutes later, clutching their overnight bags and an attaché case full of cash, Art and Annabelle thanked the driver and watched him drive away. They were on their own, and their great adventure was about to begin!

After a great roll in the hay the next morning, Hollister and Annabelle called a taxi, checked out of their motel, and went back to Rosewood Center. Leaving their small hand luggage in a couple of coin-operated lockers, they went in search of another kind of roll, the rich, aromatic, frosted cinnamon buns they'd noticed for sale by one of the food court vendors. Accompanied by fresh coffee and orange juice, the buns provided a great breakfast. Art reflected that if, as a mortal, he ate too much, he might soon find himself bulging out of his clothes. That was a consideration, of course, but a worry on this delicious day, nah!

They went next to a department store, where they purchased 4 pieces of durable luggage, each of which rolled on hard rubber balls the size of a golf ball. They judged that, fully-packed, those four pieces, plus the three small ones they already had, would pretty well fill the trunk of their new Chrysler.

Proceeding on that theory, Art and Annabelle picked-up their purchases from the day before, packed them away, then kept on shopping for other stuff until their luggage was full. Their new coats they wore. After a late lunch, they hauled their bags to the mall entrance and, accompanied by all their stuff, took a cab to the Chrysler dealership.

Their salesman was all cheerfulness as he gave Hollister his various documents, and two sets of car keys. He smiled even more broadly when Hollister handed him an envelope containing 20 fifty dollar bills. After that, the salesman even helped Art and Annabelle load their luggage into their new car, and came up with a couple of hangers so they could hang their coats in the back seat. Finally ready to roll, Hollister waved to the salesman and drove off.

To Annabelle's surprise, Hollister drove for exactly 2.2 miles, then pulled into a large parking lot. They were back at Rosewood Center. Leaving his puzzled companion in the car, Hollister proceeded to the mall entrance, went in, and after 5 minutes emerged again. As he returned to the Chrysler, Art held up his purchases to relieve Annabelle's curiosity. He was clutching the latest edition of the *Rand McNally Road Atlas,* and a felt-tipped highlighting pen for marking routes on msps.

Back in the car, Hollister pored over the atlas for a while, then mumbled "let's see, now. We're in Utica, in upstate New York, and we want to end up this part of our travels in Madison, Wisconsin. Okay, we'll head northeast a while and see where that leads us."

"Northeast, Art? The last time I checked, Wisconsin was due west of here."

"That's if you want to travel as the crow flies. After 60 years in the flatlands of TNW, I want to see some mountains and some ocean and some trees and some birds and some animals and stuff like that. When we get to the business part of this trip we'll see airplanes and airports and big cities and so on, but even if it's not really the season, let's smell some roses!"

"If that's what you want to do, Art, it's fine with me. I spent much of my last life on Earth in flat, dusty parts of this country, and I'm sure I'll like most of the places you want to see just as much as you will. Tell you what. If you ever want me to navigate for you, fine. I'll be happy to do it. Otherwise, I'll go where you want to go, and I'm sure I'll enjoy the ride."

For the next couple of weeks, Art and Annabelle wandered here and meandered there. They saw the Green Mountains of Vermont and the White Mountains of New Hampshire. From Portland, Maine they viewed the mighty Atlantic Ocean, and in that city they feasted on Maine Lobster. Next, they headed south to Boston, did the tourist bit and saw the sights.

Finally they turned west, then south, then west again on perhaps the most famous of early super highways, the storied Pennsylvania Turnpike. When they neared something of interest, they stopped and visited it, whether it was an intriguing antique shop in a small town, or the historic battlefields of Gettysburg, where in an earlier lifetime Union forces under Hollister's command had engaged in mortal combat against the grey and butternut clad legions of the Confederacy. His name hadn't been Hollister then, of course, but the Battle of Gettysburg was an indelible part of his past.

As they left Pennsylvania, and began the dreary trek across northern Ohio and Indiana, Art and Annabelle enlivened things a bit by telling each other about their most recent lives on Earth, and what they'd been doing in TNW since then. Hollister told Annabelle about his earlier days, about how he had met Amy Lawrence back in 1913, been her lover for 20 years, but never married her.

When describing his years in TNW, Hollister didn't hold back, either. He admitted that like just about every other resident of TNW, he'd had a number of liaisons over the years, some friendly, some essentially meaningless. Art went on to tell Annabelle about his twice yearly reunions with Amy Lawrence and, of course, about the happy camaraderie he'd enjoyed as part of the Frolicsome Four.

Finally, Art shared with Annabelle the fact that he was, for all intents and purposes, one of the Great Minds. He conferred with them frequently, played golf with them on a regular basis, and now was on a visit to Earth which was fully endorsed by the Great Minds. His current mission, to implement the publication of a book about TNW, and to promote that book's distribution, was one of the Great Minds' two forthcoming gifts to Earth.

The other was the Planet Earth Population Control Project, or whatever one wished to call it. The first project was to put human minds at rest over what kind of life-after-death future lay ahead of them. The second project was a last ditch attempt to enhance the quality of human life, by reducing the number of humans who would be inhabiting the Earth at any one time.

"I'm heading to Madison to try to find an old friend of mine. When I first met him, David Curtis was 32 and I was 59. Our acquaintance was a short but extremely poignant one. Now I'm a perpetual age 30, and Dave must be about 47. Before I approach anyone else about my project, I want to talk to Dave. When I first come face to face with him it's bound to be quite a shock, and perhaps you can help me figure out a way to reduce the situation's trauma for both of us.

"Now, you know just about all there is to know about me. Let's hear about you."

"I promised you, Art, that someday I'd tell you how old I was in 1900. By the middle of that year I had lived 58 years, and had been dead almost two years. But, I'm getting ahead of myself.

"I was born in 1840. My parents were homesteaders in what was to become Kansas Territory in 1854, and officially become the State of Kansas in 1861. The guerrilla raids and fighting prior to Kansas' statehood, over whether Kansas would be a slave state or a free state, made living there dangerous and often downright miserable. Kansas entered the Union as a free state on January 29, 1861. Six months later I celebrated my 21st birthday by leaving the place for good.

"I'd acquired a certain amount of nursing skill by working in a small town hospital, and with the outbreak of the Civil War I wanted to serve my country in some meaningful way. So, with the war only a few months old, I volunteered to work as a nurse, caring for the war's victims. As I was young, strong and willing, I soon became involved in field hospital work, assisting surgeons whose skills ranged from quite expert to outright butchery.

"There were times, frankly, when the whole thing became so nauseating that I considered giving it up. I'd take a break for a few days, then go right back into the thick of it.

"Toward the end of the war I met and fell in love with Colonel Charles Thompkins, U.S. Army Medical Corps. Charles had studied in the best medical schools then available, and at 29 was a highly competent surgeon. Shortly after Lee's surrender at Appomattox, Charles was mustered out of the service, and he and I were married.

"Charles and I settled in Baltimore, where he soon established a successful and lucrative medical practice. We had four children, two sons and two daughters, lived in a large and comfortable home, usually employed a staff of three servants, and had a pleasant and active social life.

"In due time the children grew up and got on with their own lives. Charles was about to retire when, in 1895, at the age of 60, his heart simply gave out, and he dropped over dead. I was left well provided for, and continued to live in what had been our family home.

"Then, in the summer of 1898, I decided to travel out west. I planned to take in the Trans-Mississippi Exhibition in Omaha, and to see if I could locate any long lost relatives in Kansas. As fate would have it, I was a passenger on the same train as the Great Minds, and died in the wreck just as they did. I was part of the group on the Baldonian space ship, and one of the pioneer residents of TNW. To this day, my room assignment is in a unit in Building A 1, just a couple of units down the hall from where the Great Minds reside.

"Over the years I've worked a lot of volunteer jobs in TNW, and for the past 15 years I've been working two months on and two months off at the Volunteer Efforts Agency on Earth. Amazingly, this is the first time I've become involved with one of TNW's special travelers to Earth, and the first time I've ventured over 75 miles from the VEA headquarters where we met.

"I'm having a great time traveling with you, and I don't miss that damn orange jump suit one bit! Look's like we're almost out of Indiana. Do you plan to mosey around the Chicago area for a while, or head on up to Madison?"

"We'll undoubtedly visit Chicago a bit later on, Annabelle, but right now let's find a motel. Tomorrow morning we'll hit the road for Badgerland. And speaking of Badgers, they're six and one so far this fall, and in three days they take on mighty Michigan at Camp Randall. That game I'd like to see!"

Chapter 21

It was about noon on Thursday when, after an uneventful trip north on Interstate Highway 90, Hollister took the U.S. 151 exit and headed into Madison. Spotting East Towne Mall on his left, he pulled into the parking lot, and parked as closely as he could to the mall entrance. Hollister and Annabelle entered the mall, and found themselves in the food court area. While Annabelle purchased lunch for the two of them, and found a suitable table, Hollister located a book store, where he bought a map of the Madison Metropolitan Area. Before returning to Annabelle, Hollister spotted a bank of telephones, consulted a telephone book and made a few notes.

"Amazingly," said Hollister, as he located Annabelle's table and joined her, "there are only two David Curtises listed in the local phone directory. Either the man I'm looking for is one of them, or he has an unlisted phone number, or he's flown the coop to parts unknown. Let's finish our food, and then make a few phone calls."

Hollister's first call, to an east side residence, went unanswered. His second was answered by a rather youngish sounding woman, and there were the sounds of one or more young children in the background. The lady obviously welcomed a chance, however brief, to converse with an adult. Hollister's open admission that he was looking for an old friend named David Curtis, who lived in Madison at one time and would now be about 47 years old, brought forth the information that her husband was an Assistant Professor of Anthropology at the University of Wisconsin, thirty years old, and until a few months earlier a resident of Seattle. So far, the young couple had met no one else in Madison named Curtis, let alone another David Curtis.

Having struck out so far, Hollister proceeded to plan B. He called directory assistance, and learned that there was another David Curtis in the area, who had an unlisted phone number. Hollister consulted the directory yellow pages, made a few further notations and one more call. Then, accompanied by Annabelle, he returned to his car.

"Somehow, Annabelle," Hollister said, "I can't help thinking that Dave Curtis is here in Madison. There's one person by that name, living somewhere around here, who has an unlisted phone number. Right now we're going to see someone who may be able to help us."

Ten minutes later, Hollister and Annabelle were in the offices of Primo Investigations, obviously a one-man operation, and talking to the proprietor, a young fellow in his mid-twenties named Mitch Johnson. Johnson invited his prospective clients to be seated, in the only two extra chairs the place had to offer, then sat down behind his desk and asked how he might be of service.

"Mr. Johnson," said Hollister, "my name is Arthur Hollister, and this is Annabelle Thompkins. We'll come right to the point. Can you obtain an unlisted Madison area phone number for us, and the address that goes with it? The man we're looking for is named David Curtis, and we assuredly mean him no harm."

Thus speaking, Hollister laid two $100 bills on Johnson's desk, but kept his hand partially covering them.

"I might be able to help you, Mr. Hollister," Johnson replied, "but if I do I'll have to be sure that the information is not put to improper use. I may be young, and I may be hungry, but I also have to live with myself. If you folks could just step out in the hall for a few minutes, I'll see what I can find out."

Hollister returned his money to his pocket, then he and Annabelle went out into the hall to wait. Ten minutes later, Johnson joined them, after locking his office door behind himself.

"The answering machine will have to hold down the fort for a while," Johnson said. "If you folks will just get in your car and follow me, I'll get in my car and lead you out to Mr. Curtis' house. I've talked to Mr. Curtis by phone, identified myself, and told him I'd like to bring somebody out to see him. I did not mention your names. The drive, by the way, will take about 25 minutes."

"Well done, Mr. Johnson," Hollister said. "If this turns out to be the gentleman I'm looking for, I'll pay you $500. If it's someone else named David Curtis, you still get the original $200 I tempted you with. I warn you in advance, if this is the right man he'll be incredibly surprised to see me.

"When we get out to his house, I think it would be best if you go to Curtis' door alone, and identify and introduce yourself, while Annabelle and I wait outside in our car. Please see for yourself whether this is a man about 47 years old, and ask him whether he owns or once owned a 1933 Duesenberg. If the answers are affirmative, please set things up so that Dave and I can have our first encounter in complete privacy. When I return to the door and give you a double thumbs up signal, Annabelle will pay you $500. Annabelle will then come inside and join us, and you can be on your way, with our sincere thanks. Who knows, we may call upon you again."

In just under half an hour, the two-car caravan had proceeded to Madison's far west side, in an area of large homes set on what appeared to be plots of about two acres. Williams pulled into the driveway of a beautiful Spanish style hacienda, two stories high, with a balcony that ran across the front at the second story level. Constructed of salmon colored brick, and complete with a tile roof, the house was truly impressive, and the well-landscaped grounds set it off perfectly.

As pre-arranged, Annabelle and Hollister parked out on the street, and waited while Johnson approached the house, rang the bell, and was subsequently admitted. About ten minutes later, Hollister and Annabelle saw Johnson approaching their car, accompanied by a man who most assuredly was not David Curtis. Hollister got out of the car to talk with the two men.

"Sir," said Johnson, "This is Mr. Curtis' driver, Paulo. Paulo will accompany you into the house to see Mr. Curtis, and will have to check to see that you are not carrying any, er, weapons. Sorry, but that's a security precaution I had to agree to. He checked me over, too, before letting me see Mr. Curtis."

"Thank you, Mr. Johnson," Hollister replied. "You've done an excellent job so far. And, given the times we live in, I can understand the safeguards."

With that, Hollister walked to the house with Paulo. Just inside the door, Paulo patted Hollister down, then led him into the living room and into the presence of David Curtis. Paulo then left the two alone.

"Mr. Curtis," said Hollister in a masterful understatement, "I suspect you'll be a bit surprised by my visit. No doubt I look sort of familiar to you, but you can't quite place me. When I last saw you, I had silver hair, was almost 60 years old, and was about to die. You were 30, full of piss and vinegar, and about to drive off in my new Duesenberg, the trunk of which contained over $100,000 in gold and currency. My name is—"

"Arthur Hollister!" David Curtis exclaimed. "I'd say this is impossible, except that you didn't say that when I met you back in 1933 during my travels through time, and I certainly owe you the same credence. Are you a ghost, come to see me after all these years, or what?"

"I'm not exactly a ghost, Dave. While I'm here on Earth I'm as mortal as you are, but I *have* spent the last 60 years or so in a place called The Next World, or TNW for short. We're all dead there, but we sure know how to live it up! I've got lots to tell you, but before I go on I'd like to signal the detective who brought us out here that everything is fine, and it's okay for my traveling companion to join us. In fact, why don't we both go out on your front stoop, give a double thumbs up signal, and then get our reunion properly underway?"

Suiting action to words, both Art and Dave went out the front door of Curtis' home, and signaled that all was okay. Soon thereafter, Annabelle had pulled the Chrysler into a parking space just off the Curtis' driveway, the detective was happily on his way, $500 richer, and the two men and the lady were all sipping iced soft drinks.

As Hollister looked around the beautifully furnished living room, he saw an elderly black and white tomcat, very much the monarch of all he surveyed, watching him carefully from what looked like a very comfortable chair. Noticing Hollister's interest in the cat, Curtis arose, walked over to the animal, scratched his head fondly, and made appropriate introductions.

"Bandit, I want you to meet an old friend of mine, Art Hollister, and his charming friend Annabelle Thompkins. Art and Annabelle, this is Bandit. I bought him on my first trip through time, from 1976 back to 1942. So, in a way, Bandit is now fifty-one years old! At any rate, if

Bandit looks and acts like he owns the place, please humor him. You might say he's entitled!"

About fifteen minutes later, Dave's charming wife Nannette, her radiant halo of blonde hair now streaked with grey here and there, returned from a shopping trip and joined the group.

"Nannette," said Dave, "You remember how I traveled back to 1933 to find you, how I met Arthur Hollister there, and how Mr. Hollister later died in a fire at his home? Well, this is Art Hollister, looking not as he did when I first met him, but as he did when he was 30 years old. Art's lovely traveling companion is Annabelle Thompkins. Both these folks have been residents of a place called The Next World for many years, but while they are here on Earth they're actually as mortal as we are. I'm sure these two have a lot to tell us, just as we have some things to share with them. Now, you're as filled-in as I am."

"It's a great pleasure to meet you both!" said Nannette. "Having traveled through time with Dave twice, first from 1933 to 1976, and later on a round trip from 1976 to 1993, I'm willing to accept what he tells me. If Dave tells me you two have been dead for years, but now you're alive and sitting here with us, I believe it, I believe it!

"One thing I ask is that when our kids get home from school, which will be about an hour from now, you let us introduce you to them as Mr. Hollister and Mrs. Thompkins, some business associates of Dave's from Illinois. Perhaps we'll have to let Craig and Nancy in on this Next World business a bit later on, but I don't think we have to rush it. I mean, uh, they still don't know that I originally met Dave when he was time traveling."

"I think you had better change one part of that story right away, Nannette," said Annabelle. "Those kids will spot in a minute that our car has New York license plates. Best you say we're from New York, which in a manner of speaking we are."

"So now, Dave," said Hollister, "tell me what's been going on in your life since I last saw you. Then I'll reciprocate, and also tell you what brought me back to Earth after all these years."

"Fair enough, Art," Dave replied. In terms of my real time here on Earth, it's been 17 years since I saw you. I brought Nannette back here with me from 1933 to 1976, where her older self, Nancy, was waiting. Nannette and I married, and Nancy lived with us until her death in 1985.

"For a few years I worked closely with Craig Donovan, the man who had invented the time machine which let me travel back to 1933. I helped him mainly in marketing activities, and was also able to contribute a few useful suggestions which led to new inventions by Donovan and his colleagues. Eventually I drifted into other business involvements, but I kept closely in touch with Donovan and his wife Marty, who were like parents to me. Donovan and Marty both died in the early 1980's, and I inherited a substantial amount from them.

"Over the years, most of my investments of time and money have turned out rather well. It's been quite an improvement over 1976, when I became burned-out at my former trade, photography, and was ready to risk all I had, which wasn't much, in an attempt to 'get rich.'

"Nannette and I have been very happy together, our children have been a delight, at least most of the time, and we're very comfortable. We've lived here for 11 years now, and for the last 6 we've had a fine Mexican couple living with us. Paulo, whom you've met, Art, and his wife Maria have been a godsend. Paulo is our chauffeur, gardener, houseman and bodyguard. Paulo's a talented mechanic and general fix-it man, too. He's never happier than when he's babying that Duesenberg you gave me.

"Maria is our housekeeper, sometime cook and a great companion to us all. Paulo and Maria have no children of their own, and we've become their family. What's really been great is that when Nannette and I have wanted to travel somewhere, we've known that our home and youngsters were in capable and entirely trustworthy hands. Okay, Art, it's your turn now."

"Well, Dave, you know how Amy and I died in that fire back in 1933. For the next 60 years, up until about two-and-a-half weeks ago, I've been residing in a great place called The Next World. Rather than roasting in hell for my sins, or trying to learn how to play a harp when my instrument has always been the piano, I've been relaxing, enjoying myself, and sometimes working on what I guess you could call public service projects.

"It's actually one of those projects that has led me back to Earth, but I'm getting ahead of my story a bit.

"You're probably wondering what became of Amy. She's fine, and we get together twice a year, a week at her place and a week at mine. In between, we each get on with our own concerns. It's a terrific situation, and it sure beats any other concept of afterlife I ever heard of.

"I had never met Annabelle until I reached Earth, but had I met her when I was young, as she appears now, I'd never have rested until she had become mine for as long as we both did live. We're having a ball traveling with each other, and expect that situation to continue until we both return to TNW. We're sure to continue seeing each other there, too, but it won't be on a daily basis."

At this point Nannette broke into the conversation. "Dave and I would be delighted to have you both as our guests for dinner tonight. If you'd like to stay with us for a while, we've got a beautiful guest room and would love to accommodate you."

Hollister and Annabelle accepted Nannette's gracious invitation, assuring her that they'd stay only a few days. Hollister also acknowledged that their staying at the Curtis home temporarily would be extremely helpful, in light of business matters he would be talking over with Dave. At this point, the noise and energy level in Dave and Nannette's home rose markedly, as their youngsters got home from school.

Dave introduced 15-year-old Craig and 13-year-old Nancy to Hollister and Annabelle. Hollister thought he saw a puzzled look pass fleetingly over young Craig's face, but he made no comment. After a few minutes of conversation, including Craig's saying that Hollister sure had a neat set of wheels, the kids headed off to their respective rooms, to study or whatever. Nannette went to inform Maria that they'd have two extra for dinner, and Dave showed Hollister and Annabelle around the house, then helped them get settled in their room.

At dinner, Hollister brought up a subject dear to his heart. "I've been following Big Ten football for years, Dave, even though my beloved Northwestern Wildcats haven't given me much to cheer about. I note, however, that the Badgers are having a great year. That Michigan game on Saturday should be something else and a half!"

"Would you like to see the game, Art? I've got some pretty good friends in the UW Athletic Department, and I think they can help me out with some tickets. If we can get four decent seats together, the kids can use our regular season tickets, and all six of us can enjoy the game. We can all ride in Nannette's van, do some tailgating before the game, and have a great time."

"I'm sure Annabelle would enjoy that immensely, Dave, and I know I would. I've got a dear friend named Bryce Wilkinson, a loyal Wisconsin grad, who has urged me to follow the Badgers this year if I want to see some winning football. Maybe, just maybe, I'll do that for the rest of the season, and of course for any bowl game Wisconsin may get invited to. You remember, of course, that it was a loss at Northwestern last fall that kept the Badgers out of a bowl."

"Of course I remember that sad occasion, Art, just as I'm sure you noticed the thumping we gave Northwestern this year! Okay, we've got a date. I give Badger football, and the great UW Marching Band, rather substantial financial support, and seldom ask for favors. When I *have* asked for something, the Badger powers that be have never let me down. I'll call Pat Richter, the Wisconsin Athletic Director, first thing tomorrow morning."

Chapter 22

On Friday morning, Hollister was up and dressed by 6:30. Wandering downstairs to the kitchen, he figured to rummage around and see if he could produce a cup of instant coffee. Instead, Hollister was greeted by a smiling Maria, who supplied him with a steaming mug of fresh-brewed java. Maria stated that breakfast would be ready at 7:15, so Hollister decided to look around the yard a bit, and see if he saw any interesting birds or flowers. Wandering around the back yard, sipping his coffee from time to time, Hollister noted several varieties of birds, including Cardinals, Blue Jays, Eastern Meadowlarks and what he was pretty sure was a Downy Woodpecker. Frost apparently had held off so far, since flowers he saw included roses, marigolds, chrysanthemums and even some dahlias.

Hollister was about to head back into the house for a refill on coffee, when to his surprise he was joined by Dave's son, Craig.

"Good morning, Mr. Hollister," Craig began. "I happened to look out the window and see you here, so I thought I'd come out and see if I could talk privately with you for a few minutes."

"Good morning to you, Craig," Hollister replied. "I assume you have something special to ask or tell me, so the floor, I mean the lawn, is yours"

"Well, Mr. Hollister, the thing is that Dad doesn't think my sister and I know about his travels in time, how he went back to 1933 and met you, and more importantly, how he met Mom and brought her back to 1976.

"Mom and Dad have never told us about those days, but Dad wrote a whole book about it. I stumbled across a few pages of the manuscript one day, when I went into Dad's den to look something up in his set of encyclopedias. I snooped around a bit, and discovered the whole text on a floppy disk. I fired up Dad's computer, made a copy of the disk for myself, and later used my own computer to read the whole story.

When I was done, I let my sister read it, too, steamy love scenes and all. Naturally I swore Nancy to secrecy, and as far as I know she hasn't spilled the beans to anyone. In a few months that won't make a lot of difference, though, since I think the book is going to be published quite soon, and everyone will know all about it after that.

"When Dad introduced you yesterday, I almost gave myself away. What puzzled me was both how you could be alive, and how you could be so young. If you had somehow survived the fire, you would be almost 120 years old now! So, I have to ask, are you a ghost?"

"No, Craig, I'm not a ghost, or a zombie, even though I *have* been dead for the last 60 years. It happens that I've been an inhabitant of a place called *The Next World*, ever since 1933, and in the last couple of years I've written a book about TNW, as we usually call it. My book, in brief, is intended to let the people of the world know where the vast majority of their souls will end up after they die, and that they really don't have anything to worry about. While I'm here on Earth, I'm as mortal as you are.

"I'm here to see whether your father might be willing and able to help me get my book published, and to see that it is properly distributed and promoted. In fact, that's what I hope to talk to your dad about today."

"I certainly wish you luck, Mr. Hollister, and I hope I'll get a chance to read your book, too! Right now it's about breakfast time, and all this walking and talking has made me hungry. Let's go in and see what Maria has for us this morning."

After breakfast, with the youngsters safely off to school, and Nannette and Annabelle happily embarked on a combined shopping and sightseeing expedition for the day, Dave and Art had a chance to settle down and talk. Before they started, however, Dave called the UW Athletic Department and secured a promise of four excellent tickets for Saturday's game.

"All right, Art," Dave began, "just what is this serious business we have to talk about?"

"Dave," Hollister replied, "I've written a book. It's called *Fear Not The Future*, and is about life in The Next World. Because of the message this book has for mankind, I think it has the potential to be just about the most important book ever published. I don't claim that my writing can hold a candle to the work of dozens of authors I could name, but none of them ever had a story like this to tell.

"Boiled down, the message is that almost everyone who dies on Earth will sooner or later end up in The Next World. All souls must have recycled at least twice. In other words, they must have been the life force in no less than three different human lifetimes, to qualify to reside in TNW for as long as they wish. Conversely, almost all souls may recycle as often as they wish.

"The only exceptions are the souls of those who could be rightly called the 'Scum of the Earth.' Those souls are merely transformed into eternal nothingness. There's no torment in store for the slime of humanity, but there's no tomorrow for them, either.

"I have the complete text of my book on this floppy disk. If you're as impressed by it as I think you will be, I hope you can steer me to somebody who will publish and promote my book.

"Talk about incredible coincidences, Art! I've written a book, too, and it's due to be published sometime next year. My book is entitled *Fires of Time*, and describes the adventures I had traveling through time. My meetings with you, in the Year 1933, are a very prominent part of the story. By the way, I still have the beautiful special group of $20 gold pieces you gave me. Every so often I visit them, and my stamp collection, in the bank vault they now occupy. I treasure the Hollister Double Eagle Collection, and want to thank you very, very much for making me such a gift.

"I, in turn, have the manuscript of my book on a floppy disk, and invite you to read it. In fact, I'll get you set up on Craig's computer, and you can read my story while I read yours. We'll take a break for lunch, of course, then continue reading this afternoon. By dinner time we'll each have a pretty good idea of the other guy's chronicle.

By the cocktail hour late that afternoon, each man had completed reading the other's manuscript. The gentlemen and their ladies sat and sipped. Dave and Nannette had margaritas, Hollister an ultra dry martini, and Annabelle a bourbon and sour. The ladies, each wearing a new dress, pronounced the day's excursion a success. Dave and Art, each dressed very casually, announced that they had formed a joint publishing venture.

"Under the circumstances, Nan, I'd have given Art anything he wanted, helped him get his book published even if I thought it was basically drivel. But I can tell you, this book of his is going to be the publishing sensation of the century, probably of the millennium! *Fear Not The Future* is going to attract more attention, sell more copies, and generate more of an uproar, than any book in the memory of man! I'll get re-fills for us, and we can all drink a toast to the most excitement to come into our lives in a long, long, time!"

The following morning, the Curtises and their guests enjoyed one of the great pleasures Madison has to offer, the Saturday Farmers Market on the Capitol Square. Late in the season as it was, the vendors still had a wide variety of apples, winter squash, potatoes, pumpkins, cheeses, meats, and bakery goods for sale, along with such special goodies as apple cider, honey, maple syrup, preserves, nut meats, wild rice, cranberries and herbal seasonings. The patrons were in good spirits. Many of them wore red, and were obviously looking forward to the big game that afternoon.

The quartet returned to Dave and Nannette's home, and dropped off their purchases. Then, having packed the back of Nannette's van with an assortment of football game and pre-game paraphernalia and supplies, and having gathered up the two Curtis children, the group headed for Camp Randall Stadium. Dave, who had rented parking space at the same location for years, knew that a spot would be waiting for them. Hollister mused that he'd soon be watching the first football game he'd attended in person in over six decades.

Maria had packed a fine selection of food for them, including sandwich steaks and hot dogs ready for grilling. Dave set up his portable grill, got the charcoal going, and supplied everyone with beer or soft drinks, plus plenty of munchies, to tide them over until he was ready to cook the main course. The group enjoyed their tailgating immensely, and soon there was just a short time until kickoff, and they all headed for the stadium.

THE NEXT WORLD

Their seats were all located on the west side of the field, in the lower deck, and between the 30 yard-line markers. Prior to that date, Wisconsin, in all its football history, had only managed home victories over Michigan twice. On that day, in a close and hard fought game, the Badgers defeated the Wolverines 13-10. Badger home games are normally topped off with a delightful performance by the great UW Marching Band, a fine Wisconsin tradition known as 'The Fifth Quarter.' On October 30, 1993, that performance never took place.

Exuberant fans from the student section at the northeast corner of the stadium set out to sweep onto the field in joyous celebration. Many of them made it, and a group of young men tried to tear down the north goal posts. Fans in the rest of the stadium watched in amusement, until the situation turned grim. Suddenly, the loud speaker announcer was trying vainly to get the people on the field to move aside to allow ambulances to reach injured fans. Over twenty people, most of them young women, had been squeezed against the rails separating the stands from an asphalt area surrounding the playing field itself. Others were crushed against the fence which encircled the field. Only when the announcer pleaded that paramedics were treating a "pulseless female non-breather," and desperately needed an ambulance for her, did the mob on the field seem to wake up and begin to disperse. Ultimately, a stream of ambulances from all over Dane County bore the victims away to various Madison Hospitals.

Although many Badger players had left the field and reached the locker room before the uncontrolled tumult began, others who had tarried behind found themselves in the role of rescuers. Badger Co-Captain Joe Panos, an offensive tackle, led the charge as he had all year, this time seeking out those who desperately needed help. Besides Panos, Badger heroes of the rescue effort included Mike Brin, Joe Rudolph, Tyler Adam, Bryan Patterson, Brent Moss and others. Although over 20 victims were transported away by ambulances, and a reported total of over 60 fans suffered injuries of varying degrees, there fortunately were no fatalities.

It was a somber crowd, indeed, which made its way home from Camp Randall Stadium on that Halloween eve.

Chapter 23

After a Sunday noteworthy for not much at all, and highlighted by passing out candy to costumed children who came around that night trick or treating, Hollister and Curtis were ready to get down to some serious business on Monday morning. The ladies asked to sit in, and the gentlemen readily agreed.

"In our slightly alcoholic euphoria Friday evening," Hollister began, "there were some very important things we failed to consider. Now, in the cold, hard light of a sober Monday morning, we had better talk about them. Anxious as I am to have my book published, I'm afraid there could be some serious risks for you and your family, Dave. I'm not talking about money, but the danger of physical harm to you and yours."

"Excuse me, Art," Curtis broke in, "but just exactly what are you referring to?"

"Suppose somebody in the God Business got so incensed over the publication of my book, and the help you gave me in accomplishing it, that they became obsessed with revenge against you or even your family. That 'somebody' could be a Bible thumping evangelist whose organization was taking in tens of millions each year from the faithful and gullible, and saw the cash spigot in jeopardy. It could be anyone in the world with a strong vested interest in maintaining the religious status quo, even the Vatican.

"History, as you know, is loaded with examples of man's inhumanity to man in the name of religion. The crusades and the Spanish Inquisition are only two of many examples. If you help me prove the truth of TNW, those whose livelihood depends on the glories of heaven versus the fire and brimstone of hell could become very upset, if you get my drift."

"History tells us," Dave said, "that certain kings and other rulers would have someone who brought them bad news put to death—kill the messenger, as it were. Now you're saying that something like that could happen to me and my family. That may shed a different light on this whole business. What do you think, Nan?"

"This is too important a project to fink out on, Dave, but we'll have to take a lot of precautions. You and I can take some chances, but we have to make sure the kids are safe. Maybe some of your 'special friends', those who remember Craig Donovan, can help us."

"That's worth looking into, Nan. If and when we feel it's necessary, I think I know someone who can help us hide the kids away where they'll be absolutely safe. We'd probably send Paulo and Maria with them, too. For right now, though, let's examine all aspects of the situation. If you have any ideas, Annabelle, be sure to let us know."

"As a matter of fact, Dave, I do have a suggestion. If the time comes when we need security people, the Volunteer Efforts Agency can bring in all the help we need from TNW. For that matter, VEA can come up with volunteers in just about any capacity you could name. Bodyguards, housekeepers, gardeners, lawyers, doctors—whatever you need. But, before we panic about anything, let's give the whole situation a great deal of careful thought."

"I think that's the right approach," said Dave. "If we work this thing right, there are all sorts of ways I can help Art, yet never get directly involved. I can steer him toward an agent, a publisher, a publicity expert, the best sales promotion people around. What I can't do is let myself get caught in the spotlight."

"Probably the first thing you had better do, Dave," Hollister said, "is have a talk with your kids. Find out whether either of them has told friends or anyone else about Annabelle's and my visit with you. See if they have told anyone at all our names. Impress on them that from this point on they must never mention us to anyone. That includes their best friends, their teachers, absolutely anyone at all. Once we've plugged those potential leaks, we can go on from there.

"One of the toughest things we'll face will be the day when we realize that the four of us can't get together in person anymore. Annabelle and I will leave here soon, and find accommodations elsewhere. Be sure you tell Maria and Paulo to forget that you had house guests from New York this fall. When we've moved on, by the way, you might tell them that the folks who weren't here thanked them both for all their courtesies.

"If you'll give us your unlisted number, we can call you from time to time, from various locations, and either transact business over the phone or arrange to meet you somewhere. There's really almost no risk right now, and won't be until my book is published. That's why we want to severely restrict the number of people who can connect us with you.

"You folks are wonderful hosts, and Annabelle and I want to thank you profusely. There's one more favor I'd like to ask right now, Dave. Do you suppose you could locate 4 tickets for me to the Ohio State game this Saturday?"

"I'll have them delivered here by messenger late this afternoon, Art. I assume you have some special plans, and I won't pry into them. Now, what's next?"

"Let's consider your own book for a minute, Dave. When it comes out, it's bound to focus a degree of attention on you. And, you *do* mention in the book that you traveled back in time, and met me in 1933. Do you think that could lead people, later on, to tie you in with me?"

"It might, Art, but let's consider the matter a bit. First, the book isn't being published with my own name on the spine. As far as the public in general is concerned, *Fires of Time* will be an obscure first novel by some guy called Gratton Coffman. Nannette and I are merely fictional characters in that novel.

"Even if some investigative reporter sees through that ruse, what can it really matter? Yes, I did meet you in 1933, and yes, I was mightily impressed by you. But, you died back there, and that was the end of it as far as I was concerned. It will be just as much a shocking surprise to me as to anyone else, it says here, when you burst upon the scene as the author of the most Earth-shaking book ever written. When you become a celebrity, and I guarantee your name will become a household word, I'll have no part in it as far as the world knows.

"You've read the story of my earlier days, and of my time travels. I like to think my adventures turned out successfully because I planned carefully, didn't rush rashly into things, and avoided trouble when I could. Without Donovan's time machine, none of it would have been possible. Of course, without Nancy and her younger self, now my dear sweet Nannette, it would have been more difficult, and essentially meaningless.

"All these ramblings are by way of saying that we should formulate our plan of attack carefully, and then carry it out. I've yacked long enough now, Art, so let's have some more input from you and the ladies."

"The input I'm going to arrange right now," said Nannette, "is lunch for all of us in about half an-hour."

"We appreciate that, Nannette," said Hollister. "Now, here's what I have in mind. If we may, Dave, we'd like to use your phone to make a couple of long distance calls. We're going to arrange to have a few folks called in from TNW. You'll never meet them, Dave, and we won't even tell you their names. Just rest assured that the presence of these individuals will be very helpful to our project.

"What I also need from you as soon as possible, Dave, is a typewritten list of names, addresses, phone and FAX numbers of the people you alluded to before—the publisher, literary agent, publicity guy and so on. We'll be in touch with these people, but will never mention your name. We may end up hiring one or more people suggested by you, or may find some on our own. In any event, we certainly appreciate your offering us your recommendations.

"Now, I'm going to share another thing with you. You already have a great deal of money. I have access to all I need while I'm here on Earth, and when I go back to TNW I won't need money. So, I'm going to channel all the proceeds from my book into one very special cause. I'm not going to tell you exactly what it is, but you can be certain it's for the benefit of humanity.

"I suggest," Hollister went on, "that after lunch we recess our talks for a while. Annabelle and I have a few things to take care of, and then I'll get back to you"

After a delicious noon repast, Art and Annabelle excused themselves and went up to their room. "I think we should check out of Chez Curtis tomorrow morning," Art said, "and find ourselves a good hotel. Even if we didn't have to consider the safety of Dave's household, it's time we give these folks some privacy."

"I quite agree," Annabelle replied. "Now, I'll be happy to call in all the people we need from TNW, once we decide who we require."

"To begin with, please arrange for Bryce Wilkinson and Alma Norton, both from Unit 414, Building KK 280, to join us. Then we'll need an excellent lawyer, good at just about everything, but whose specialty is contracts and intellectual property.

"I'll finish my present want list with a couple of really special young men. They need to be hand-to-hand combat experts, proficient with all manner of weapons and explosives, qualified fixed wing and helicopter pilots and excellent drivers. These men should be tough, intelligent and personable, and they should be equally at home in fatigues, business suits or evening wear. These guys could be former Green Berets, Navy SEALs or similar specialists.

"Please be sure that VEA provides these two with proper driver's licenses, pilot's licenses, weapons permits, passports and other documents they need. If VEA has an arsenal, please let these two select an assortment of weapons they feel comfortable with, along with weapons some of the rest of us may decide to carry, and see to it that those weapons reach here at the same time as the two men do. Now, have I left anyone out?"

"We might need a good accountant later on, and perhaps an appointment secretary and general assistant. Let's wait on those, and if we find we need one or both, or anyone else for that matter, I can have them here within 48 hours. Now, who goes where?"

"Just have the Volunteer Efforts Agency process my personnel request. Long before those people get to

Earth, we'll have selected a hotel and checked in. We'll get rooms for everybody, on the same floor as our own room. Alma and Bryce can share a room, likewise the two security types. The lawyer will have a room of his own. When we get the names of the three new men from VEA, I'll have their reservations put in their own names.

"And now, while you make the call to New York, I'll scout up Dave and see if I can arrange a special treat for us!"

Half an hour later the special treat began. With Hollister at the wheel, and Nannette beside him to navigate, Dave and Annabelle sat happily in the back seat. For two hours on a glorious sunny afternoon, seeing the sights of Madison and catching what fall color remained to be seen, the four rode in the magnificent 1933 Duesenberg which had once belonged to Arthur Hollister.

Chapter 24

On Thursday afternoon, Annabelle opened the door of the hotel room she shared with Hollister, and admitted five people she had never seen before. When one of the men rushed forward to grasp Hollister's hand, and the lady then jumped into Hollister's arms and gave him a big kiss, Annabelle knew she'd just been bypassed by, and would soon meet, Bryce Wilkinson and Alma Norton. Next, a distinguished looking, grey-haired gentleman who looked to be in his early 40's, old by TNW standards, stepped up to Annabelle, bowed slightly, and introduced himself as Howard Burns, attorney-at-law.

Annabelle had sometimes wondered if she would recognize a combination of handsome and deadly in a man if she ever encountered it. At this moment she met a double dose of those qualities, as Brad Keaton, a former U.S. Navy SEAL, and Lyle Porter, a former U.S. Army Special Forces Green Beret, politely introduced themselves, then stood at parade rest waiting for the opportunity to meet Hollister.

After shaking hands with Howard Burns, Hollister turned to meet his two security men. Although Hollister normally discouraged anyone from calling him "sir," he knew instinctively that these two would prefer to address him that way, and would feel uncomfortable if told not to do so. "Ah, well," he thought, "so be it." Shaking their hands, he welcomed them aboard. Hollister had asked the hotel to send up extra chairs, so everyone had a place to sit. After making sure that everyone had met everyone else, Hollister called the informal meeting to order.

"I'm glad to see you all, and hope you had a pleasant trip in from New York. We're all here because we have a mission to accomplish, on behalf of TNW, and for the benefit of the people of the Planet Earth. We're all residents of The Next World, where as you know the afterlife surpasses anything any of us ever dreamed of. The Earth's populace, however, is under all manner of misconceptions as to what life after death is really like. Everywhere you turn, people have different ideas about the afterlife, or whether there is one at all.

"TNW has been in operation for over 94 years, yet virtually no one here on Earth knows anything about it. Even the lowest scum of humanity, those with nothing more to look forward to under most religious beliefs than roasting in the fiery furnace, or swimming in liquid shit for all eternity, will be relieved to learn that what really faces them after they die is simply eternal nothingness.

"As what I expect will be my major contribution at TNW, and a major reassurance for humanity, I've written a book entitled *Fear Not The Future,* telling the whole story of TNW, from its inception to the present. I've brought the manuscript here to the Earth, where our mission is to see that the manuscript becomes a book, and that the book is widely distributed and read throughout the civilized world. The more the book is publicized, on radio, on television, in newspapers, in magazines, in literary journals, in movie theaters and the like, the more copies will sell and the more people will learn the story of TNW.

"There are groups and individuals, those with a vested interest in what I call the 'God Business,' who might try to stop publication of *Fear Not The Future* if they knew it was in the offing. One way or another we have to outthink, outflank and outmaneuver those who may try to stop us. American freedom of the press is on our side, but we face some tough hurdles.

"An author's usual procedure is to submit a synopsis and some sample chapters to a publishing firm, or perhaps to several such firms at once, in what is clearly identified as a simultaneous submission. Either the publishers reject the submission, or they offer the author a contract. When an author employs a literary agent, and the agent is a good one with excellent contacts, the chances of a decent manuscript's acceptance generally increase. All of these procedures take time, sometimes wasting months or years.

"Another possible way to go about this would be to find a hungry book printing plant, and offer the operators a lot of money. They'd have to agree to lease us their facilities for long enough to ensure that we could produce, say, an initial run of 100,000 copies in trade paperback format. Furthermore, we'd have an ironclad contract allowing us to renew our lease for an indefinite period.

"As a third alternative, we could purchase a book printing plant outright. We would staff either a leased plant or a purchased one entirely with personnel from TNW. Once an output of finished books began, we'd lease trucks and, using TNW personnel as drivers, move the books to warehouses around the country, which would later become our distribution points.

"We'd plan and proceed very carefully. When the big day came, we'd follow 'instant distribution' with an advertising blitz that would send people flocking to bookstores.

"There's much, much more, but right now I'd like some questions and input from the rest of you."

The first question came from Bryce Wilkinson. "Obviously we're just the advance party of TNW people, Art, but can you tell each of us, briefly, exactly what you have in mind for us?"

"Exactly, no, but generally, yes," replied Hollister. "Between us, we're going to figure out how to get this thing done, then do it. As needs for additional TNW volunteers arise, Annabelle will coordinate with Volunteer Efforts Bureau to get the people we need, when and where we need them.

"You, Bryce, will be my right-hand man, and will have plenty to do. I also feel that your input to the project will be invaluable. Annabelle will take care of all kinds of details to help things go smoothly. Mr. Burns will take care of all legal matters and contract negotiations. He'll also seek out trustworthy Earthlings who will carry on our project after most of us have returned to TNW.

"Mr. Keaton and Mr. Porter are our security people. Should we opt to travel by chartered aircraft, either fixed-wing or helicopter, these gentlemen are qualified to be our pilots. We can't travel instantly here, the way we do in TNW, but we'll manage."

Howard Burns arose. "Given our situation, I'd like to make some suggestions. First, let's get ourselves some office space, and set a World's record on how fast we get it furnished, equipped and operational. I see no reason why that can't be here in Madison. If you have no objections, I'll handle the details. Second, I think we should buy a book manufacturing plant outright, somewhere in southern Wisconsin. We can set Bryce to finding out what's available, while Annabelle has a couple of printing and publishing experts brought in from TNW, to help us make the right choice of facilities. Third, I'd like to seek out and put under contract a leading Earthling literary agent. This person would be primed to pick up our ball and run with it, once we had made the initial publication and distribution of *Fear Not The Future* an accomplished fact."

"Am I glad TNW sent you to us!" Hollister exclaimed. "With you on the team, we can't lose! By all means get on with the office space matter, and the literary agent search. While you're at it, see if you can find us an outstanding publicist, too. I have a list of contacts suggested by a friend of mine, and I'll pass those along to you.

"Nonetheless, please broaden your search as you feel necessary, and see where it leads. During the screening process, please make sure you find people who are essentially agnostics, ready to wait and see what if anything an afterlife may consist of.

"Don't tell anyone exactly what we're up to. Just tantalize those whom you consider 'finalists' with the modest claim that this will truly be the opportunity of a lifetime for the people we select. I think we should pay the publicist appropriate fees for services performed, and offer the agent 10% of the gross on every deal he negotiates for us. The agent will probably become a millionaire many times over for his efforts.

"Annabelle will help you with any financial matters, obtain any other staff people we need for the office, and generally be in charge of logistics."

"There's something I'd like to suggest," said Alma. "Suppose I set out to feel the pulse of the religious community on this matter. I could travel around the United States, and possibly also visit several foreign countries, and talk with a cross section of religious leaders. I'd seek meetings with parish priests, bishops, television evangelists, protestant ministers, Jewish rabbis and so on, whomever I could converse with in private, and without a lot of hassle. Sometimes I'd travel alone, sometimes with Bryce, and maybe occasionally accompanied by one of our security men.

"During the course of talks with these people, I'd always pose one hypothetical question. What would they do, or at least want to do, if someone were about to prove, beyond a shadow of a doubt, that life after death was nothing like anyone thought, and had no religion-related aspects at all?

"There's an old joke about the reporter who went around asking people which human condition posed the greatest problem, ignorance or apathy. The reply he received most frequently was 'I don't know and I don't care!' Maybe human ignorance and apathy will help us."

"That's an interesting idea, Alma," Hollister commented, "and perhaps we can use it, or a modification of it."

"Just in case we have to defend the printing plant," injected Lyle Porter, "you might look for one which has a fair amount of empty land around it, and which is or can be surrounded with heavy chain link fence, topped with barbed wire. As an immediate step, I suggest that you make at least 6 copies of the computer disc of your manuscript, and distribute them to an assortment of safe points around the country. At least two of those should be bank vaults."

"Thank you, Lyle," said Hollister. "Your points are well taken. You and Brad are free to go now. Please check at the front desk for messages each morning at eight and each evening at five. In the meantime, unless you have something else to tell us now, you two are on your own until we need you."

"There is one other matter, sir," Brad Keaton said. "I've located a privately operated indoor rifle and pistol range not far from here, and would like to take our entire group there tomorrow morning for some weapons training and target practice. They can accommodate us, as long as I call them back later today to confirm."

"I admire your initiative, Brad," Hollister replied. I guess we really don't have any other conflicting plans tomorrow, and what you suggest seems like a good idea. Please arrange things as necessary. We'll all meet in the lobby at 9:00 in the morning, and place ourselves in your hands for the day."

After the security men had left, Hollister invited the others to join him for dinner, in the hotel's best diningroom. Over dinner, Hollister asked Burns to proceed with the office space matter first thing the following week. Once he had that in hand, he was to begin his search for a literary agent and a publicist. Hollister asked Burns to get back to him with a progress report the following Wednesday morning.

Following their meal, Burns excused himself, saying he wanted to catch that evening's episode of *L. A. Law* on TV. The remaining quartet lingered over an after dinner drink, during which Hollister invited the other three to join him for the Wisconsin-Ohio State football game that Saturday.

Later, the four adjourned to Hollister's room. Once there, Hollister again thanked Alma for volunteering to elicit comments from various religious leaders. He pointed out, however, three drawbacks to Alma's original idea. First, it would take too long. Second, it would require Alma's absence for extended periods, and sometimes tie up other group personnel as well. Third, and most important, it could spill the beans! If two or more of the people she interviewed happened to compare notes, who knew where that could lead?

As an alternative, Hollister suggested that Alma send word back to Thelma in TNW, asking her to conduct a poll there, among appropriate TNW residents. He pointed out that the same type of pulse feeling could be accomplished, much more rapidly because it could be done over the phone for the most part, and in complete security. Alma could simply phrase her questions along the lines of "What would have been your reaction, while you were living on Earth, had you learned about TNW, and that it's existence was about to be revealed to the whole world?" Alma readily agreed that Hollister's approach made more sense, even though she would have enjoyed some world traveling.

    The group then proceeded with other business for the rest of the evening, but is was primarily "monkey business!"

Chapter 25

On Friday morning, after a couple of hours of general handgun instruction and familiarization, Brad Keaton issued personal weapons to Hollister and his group. Hollister and Wilkinson selected 9 mm Beretta automatics, Howard Burns chose a .38 caliber Smith & Wesson revolver, and the two ladies selected .32 caliber Browning automatics.

After lunch, the group moved to the firing range, where they actually loaded and fired their weapons. It would be overstating it to say that the two security men were awed by their students' scores, but they were rather impressed.

The best shot among the men turned out to be Howard Burns, the lawyer, who finally admitted that during his younger years he'd been an olympic medalist in target shooting. At 50 feet, in slow fire, Burns could put 6 rounds into a two-inch circle more often than not. The others could best be described as "adequate" shots, who would benefit greatly from further instruction and range time.

At the end of the range session, the instructors collected all the guns, promising to return them to their new owners later that evening, cleaned, loaded and ready for use if necessary. Realizing that their use of firearms against other human beings would, in all likelihood, presage a bad ending to a desperate situation, the group sincerely hoped that such a time would never come.

The next day, a capacity crowd watched the Badgers play the Ohio State Buckeyes to a standstill, only to end up in a 14-14 tie after their try for a game-winning field goal was blocked. Bryce Wilkinson, sitting in the stands with Alma, Annabelle and Art, enjoyed the game immensely. It was the first time he'd been to a Wisconsin football game since the homecoming game in 1926, when the Badgers downed the Iowa Hawkeyes 20-10.

The following morning, sports analysts pointed out in their Sunday newspaper articles that Wisconsin could still go to the Rose Bowl, but only if two weeks hence, for starters, they beat Illinois while Michigan defeated Ohio State. Given that not impossible chain of events, the Big Ten Championship would then be decided yet another two weeks later, in Tokyo, Japan. Wisconsin would have to defeat Michigan State, always a tough opponent for them, before a crowd of mostly Japanese fans who really didn't understand American football, but who would fill the stands and whoop it up, anyhow.

Amazingly, everything went perfectly for the Badgers. Knowing that if they defeated Michigan State in Tokyo they would tie Ohio State for the Big Ten Crown, and go to Pasadena as the Big Ten representatives in the Rose Bowl, the Badgers played their best game of the year, and defeated the Spartans 41-20.

Sandwiched around football games, Hollister and his crew accomplished an awful lot. Howard Burns found them an entire floor of office space, complete with excellent furnishings, which the belly-up former tenants had simply left to the landlords in lieu of rent they were unable to pay. A week later, using the company name Totally New & Wonderful, they were in business. Staffed with additional personnel brought in from TNW, including two printing plant experts and a gentleman who had been a giant in the book publishing world, the operation was off and running!

Totally New soon located a suitable book publishing facility, purchased it, staffed it, ordered in ample stocks of paper, ink and other supplies, and got ready to roll the presses. The experts persuaded Hollister that a book of the stature of *Fear Not The Future* should be bound in hardcover, and dressed in a beautiful and impressive dust jacket as well. They then set up a first-rate bindery operation, capable of handling an enormous quantity of hardcover books.

Everything stopped for a whopper of a Christmas party, and a week later for a New Year's Eve party. Hollister, Wilkinson, Annabelle and Alma were in Madison for Christmas, but along with Dave and Nannette Curtis and another seventy thousand or so Wisconsin fans, they spent New Year's Day in California. When the Badgers defeated the UCLA Bruins 21-16, winning their first Rose Bowl game ever, loyal Badgers everywhere rejoiced!

Chapter 26

Each floor of the office building in which the Hollister Group had leased space had it's own large meeting room, with seating for up to 200 people. As of early January 1994, 126 souls from TNW were employed by Totally New & Wonderful, and on the morning of January 5th all but three attended a meeting called by Hollister. The missing trio were guards on duty at the printing plant, whom Hollister had briefed privately the previous afternoon.

"Good morning, everybody," Hollister began. "For those few of you I haven't met personally, I'm Art Hollister. I'll take the blame or the credit, as the case may be, for the fact that you're all here on Earth for a while. On behalf of TNW, we're here to print and distribute a book I wrote about The Next World. Called *Fear Not The Future*, the book will tell the people of Earth about the afterlife that really awaits the vast majority of them.

"Our plan is to produce a million copies of the book, and quietly move them to distribution points around the United States, Canada, the UK, Australia and New Zealand. We know there will be great demand for the book in other countries, but that will be handled in Phase Two, Phase Three and so on.

"As most of you know, the presses start up this afternoon. All of our equipment has been tested, and is ready to go. All the plates we need are standing, and the first sets have been locked on the presses and made ready. While our two large single color presses produce the six 32-page signatures of text, our 4-color press will turn out the dust jackets. Soon the bindery folks will be turning out finished books at a rate of some 250,000 copies per week.

"All of you were briefed on the importance of security on this project before you left TNW. There's no way I can over stress how important that is. If the wrong Earthlings heard about this book, they might resort to sabotage, terrorism or even murder to try to prevent it. We're most vulnerable right now, and for the next month or so. So, please, don't talk to anyone about this project. Just do your jobs, and take pleasure in work well done. If you encounter anything suspicious, please let our security personnel know about it at once.

"Now, let's move on to another subject. Once we've announced our book, and distributed enough copies so that no one can stop our news from spreading, the entire situation will change. We'll be involved in a big time publicity campaign, and people from TNW will be in great demand by members of the media, including press representatives of established religions.

"Those of you who wish to travel around and help spread the news will be free to do so. Those of you who simply want to visit friends or relatives, do some sight seeing or whatever will be free to do that, subsidized by a grateful TNW. Those of you who want to return to TNW right away will be accommodated.

"There's one thing none of you knows yet, but which I'm going to share with you now. We're all like visitors in a foreign land, whose visas are eventually going to expire. With only a couple of exceptions, all of us must be back in TNW by June 1st of this year. We were processed that way when we left TNW, and there's no changing it. So, if any of you has notions of staying on Earth the quick and easy way, instead of recycling, forget it. When your visas expire, so will you.

"We appreciate all of your efforts, and thank you profusely."

After lunch, Hollister met in his office with Burns, Wilkinson, Annabelle and Alma. Hollister made a quick phone call, then turned to his guests. "Well, my friends, the presses are rolling! Let's open that bottle of Champagne we've been chilling for the last couple of hours, and drink a toast to *Fear Not The Future*!"

Once everyone had sipped the celebratory libation, they settled down to talk business. Alma's report about the informal polling Thelma had done back in TNW was first.

"Thelma sends word," said Alma, "of an overwhelmingly ho-hum attitude. Almost no one she reached would have felt strongly enough about the story of TNW to try to keep the news bottled up.

These people are, or rather were, engaged in preaching the 'Word' as they understood and interpreted it. If the 'Word' changed dramatically, they'd have had to modify their messages or give up preaching.

"Man is, after all, a very adaptable creature. Preachers being no exception, most of them thought they'd have shifted their focuses more toward improving the human lot here on Earth. That would have included more emphasis on the need to preserve and protect our environment, and the discouragement of irresponsible human breeding. God wouldn't have been left out of the picture, but His overall role might have been de-emphasized somewhat."

"If we extrapolate those findings," said Wilkinson," and apply them to our own project, we're probably in pretty good shape. Human inertia being what it is, the chances are slimmer each day that someone will mount a major effort against us, even if information on what we're doing should leak out.

"We are, after all, merely engaged in spreading the truth about the hereafter. Rather than as a security problem per se, I'm beginning to perceive this as a public relations challenge."

"So now, Chief," asked Annabelle, "what's next?"

"You need," said Hollister, "to finalize arrangements to ship copies of our book to warehouse distribution points in the world's major English-speaking countries. First, however, get all the help you can from Irv Wallman, the former book publisher who's running our book manufacturing facility.

"Then, with as much guidance from Irv as you need, coordinate your efforts with Howard. Work out when books will actually be moved to stores, and who will move them there. The book will have a $19.95 cover price. If we prime the pump by giving leading book stores in selected cities 3 free copies to start, we'll virtually force them to stock the book. They'll be supplied, of course, with a toll-free number from which they can order more books at a standard trade discount of 40% off the cover price.

"Once our publicity campaign is cranked up, we quit giving away free books and settle down to filling a flood of orders. Actually, we'll have book distribution services climbing all over each other, bidding to handle that chore for us. Working with Irv, Bryce and Howard will select outfits that best meet our needs.

"As the public comes to accept our message, we may work out a deal with an honest Earthling publishing house to take over all aspects of the book's publication and distribution. Or, we can turn over general supervision of the whole operation to the most trustworthy Earthling I know, David Curtis. Dave would select a qualified plant manager, who in turn would staff our facility with competent Earthling workers, and keep things running smoothly. The plant would have to pay salaries, of course, and contend with taxes, government regulations and the like. Even at that, the profits should be enormous.

"Dave would see to it that those profits were funneled into a tax-free foundation, which Howard and Bryce will establish and staff with some very special, very dedicated Earthlings.

"Additional funds to swell the foundation's coffers would come from the sale of movie and TV rights to the TNW story, plus licensing and a whole lot more. I get so enthused thinking about it that I'm sorry we won't be around to be a part of it, except at the very beginning.

"Now, Howard, have you and Bryce located a literary agent and publicist for us? It's time we start getting acquainted with them, and vice-versa."

"Art," Howard replied, "Bryce and I have been very fortunate. After following-up a number of leads, we've found two extra-special husband and wife teams, each of which heads up a large, well-staffed and extremely successful agency.

"Leon Davis is one of the best literary agents in the business, while his wife Kristin is a dynamite talent agent. Esther Fauerbach is one of the most effective and persuasive publicists in the country, while her husband Herman is a terrific public relations guy. They say Herman could charm the pants off the Statue of Liberty!"

"What's more, each of these outfits is ready to work with us, even though we couldn't tell them exactly what we were up to. I won't say we laid it on with a trowel, but Bryce mentioned in passing that the bricklaying experience he had one summer on a long ago construction job did come in awfully handy!"

"Good work, guys!" Hollister said, a wide smile on his face. "We're likely to have work for both halves of both teams before we're done. Their only problem will be that once they've worked on our projects, everything else they ever tackle will seem about as exciting as cold mashed potatoes!"

"Just what is this mysterious foundation you mentioned?" Alma asked.

"The foundation," replied Hollister, "will be called something like 'The World Population Studies Foundation,' or perhaps something even more obscure. The foundation's purpose will be to discourage irresponsible human breeding. Overt activities supported by the foundation will include such things as the widespread distribution of birth control drugs and devices, and the dissemination of birth control information to as much of the world's populace as possible.

"Since the last thing the world needs is unwanted children, free, safe abortion on demand will be made readily available. Those who attempt to interfere with this service will, shall we say, be vigorously thawrted.

"Human sterilization will be strongly encouraged, along with the premise that when a woman has given birth to two live children, that's her quota. Slogans such as 'Small Families Live Better,' and 'Every Child Deserves A Father,' will be widely publicized and, hopefully, popularized.

"Covert activities will involve any and all safe, available means to reduce reproduction by those elements of humanity among whom irresponsible and excessive breeding is currently the norm. TNW has a program on this which will begin taking effect in a generation or so.

The foundation, on the other hand, will begin working on the matter immediately.

"Our strongest adversaries will be the Catholic Church, and certain other organized religions. Our real enemy, however, is human stupidity. What all too many people refuse to acknowledge is that unless the overpopulation juggernaut is derailed, all other efforts to genuinely improve the lot of humankind are exercises in futility.

"And that, my friends, pretty well describes the purpose of the foundation. My book's profits will go a long way toward supporting the foundation's work, but I have another card up my sleeve. I'll tell you about that a little later on, after we work out some of the details."

Chapter 27

During the next month, things went remarkably well. The printing plant, now up and running, turned out slightly more than the targeted one million copies of *Fear Not The Future*. Truckloads of the book rolled to selected distribution points throughout the U.S. and Canada, while air freight shipments, expensive though they were, moved copies to the U.K., Australia and New Zeeland. Agents throughout nearly all the English-speaking world were ready to effect rapid distribution of the book, even though at that point they knew neither its title nor its subject matter.

The small but potentially very effective security force remained ready for just about anything, but ended up having little to do. Apart from screening visitors, and turning away salesmen prepared to make cold calls at the printing plant, the 12-man force there found its greatest problem to be overcoming boredom. Brad Keaton and Lyle Porter served as security people at the Totally New & Wonderful offices, and as bodyguards when necessary. Should both men be needed for bodyguard duties, men from the guard force at the printing plant were prepared to fill in for them at the Totally New & Wonderful offices.

Once a million copies of *Fear Not The Future* had been safely shipped, Hollister instructed the printing plant to continue printing more. Then, finally, Hollister felt safe in calling the important meeting he'd been looking forward to. When that meeting took place, on the morning of February 10, 1994, those present included Hollister's main colleagues, along with Leon and Kristin Davis, literary and talent agents, respectively, and Esther and Herman Fauerbach, publicist and PR specialist, respectively. Each couple had received, along with airline tickets provided by Totally New & Wonderful, two copies of *Fear Not The Future,* with instructions to read the book on their flights to Madison.

Calling the meeting to order, Hollister formally introduced everyone present, then got down to the business at hand.

"This, my friends, is the day we've been waiting for. We've printed over a million copies of *Fear Not The Future,* and delivered them safely to warehouses throughout most of the English-speaking world. Now we're ready to tell the world our story. All of you have read my book. If everything goes according to our expectations, millions of others will soon be clamoring to do so.

"Leon, the only rights you don't have to offer are first publication rights. Everything else is wide open, and I modestly expect this will be the hottest property you ever handle.

"Kristin, I have in mind for you the most exciting project a talent agent ever undertook. I'll tell you more about that a bit later.

"Esther, we're ready to take off the wraps, and let everyone know about The Next World. I know that you'd have liked to have months to prepare a media blitz, but that simply could not be. Now, however, the sky's the limit. You can get started from here, today, and within a day or so have your whole staff involved.

"Herman, you have a tremendous challenge facing you, and from what I've heard you're the man for the job.

What you need to do is persuade those in the 'God Business' to accept life in the hereafter as it really is, not as various individuals have imagined it over the years. Organized religions will no longer be able to frighten people into being good, or into making major financial contributions with an eye toward saving their own souls. The idea of a 'Last Judgement' is basically a lot of hooey. Only the complete scum of the Earth are denied a place in TNW, and even they are simply processed into nothingness.

"There's a great deal of good the various religious organizations can do in this world, and we hope you can persuade them to get on with it, rather than wasting time and resources fighting what is both true and inevitable.

"Now," Hollister concluded, "I'd like to hear from each of you, and see what you think about all this."

"Just since you addressed me a few minutes ago," said Leon Davis, "I've thought of half a dozen markets I can sell this to. In several situations, I expect vigorous competitive bidding between interested parties. If *Fear Not The Future* doesn't prove to be *the* hottest literary property of all time, I miss my guess. I want to thank you wholeheartedly for inviting me to be part of this. I won't let you down."

"My only problem, Art," Esther Fauerbach remarked, "is that there are only 24 hours in a day, and this 45-year-old body of mine absolutely insists on 6 of them for sleep. Just about all of the rest of the time, I'm yours. After you've finished your sixth appearance on a major TV talk show, your twelfth interview by one of the top print reporters and your twenty-fourth book-signing at a major bookseller's establishment, you may wish I hadn't done such an effective job. Of course, there will be press conferences, radio call-in shows and the like as well."

"I like a challenge, Art," said Herman Fauerbach, "and you're certainly handing me one! I'll do my best to unruffle the feathers of those who had a vested interest in espousing the traditional concepts of heaven and hell. Even at that, I wouldn't want to tackle the challenge you face."

"Which particular challenge is that, Herman?" Hollister asked."

"Why, proving to the multitudes that you are who you say you are, not some kind of phony."

"I've thought about that, Herman, and I think I have the answer. Even if I fail, though, I can bring in any number of people from TNW who can supply proof positive of who they are. Without going into a lot of detail, let's just say it would involve fingerprinting, or perhaps DNA matching."

"If you are waiting for me to add something, Mr. Hollister," said Kristin Davis, "all I can say is that you'll have to tell me a lot more. I'm a talent agent, expert in negotiating fat contracts for talented, and sometimes not so talented, clients. So far, all you've done is make me curious."

"All right, Kristin, I guess now is as good a time as any to fill you in. My book will, I feel sure, earn a great deal of money. After paying our expenses, including fees and commissions to the four of you, there should be millions of dollars left over. These monies will go to a tax-free foundation, whose ostensive purpose is to study human population, but whose real objective is to curtail human population growth, for the benefit of mankind and of the Earth. I don't want any of you publicizing the foundation and its goals, but it's important that you all know about it. It's particularly important to you Kristin, for reasons I'm about to explain.

"Suppose, just suppose, that we could bring certain very special performers, sports figures, even a few carefully selected politicians, back to Earth for one great return engagement. On shows televised worldwide, people could watch the likes of FDR, Mark Twain, Will Rogers, Amelia Earhart, Lucille Ball, Jack Benny and yes, even Elvis! The shows could be put on before live audiences in huge amphitheaters, where those watching in person would put down a thousand dollars apiece, or more, for the privilege. The possibilities are endless. You'd have to work closely with a talent agent from TNW, and all prospective performers would have to be informed of the cause to which the proceeds of their performances would go. If they didn't like the idea, they could simply pass. So, how does that grab you?"

"Now I understand why you need me, Mr. Hollister," Kristin Davis replied. "You weren't kidding when you hinted that this is the opportunity of a lifetime. Just so I have this straight, are you talking about a few specials, a series or what?"

"By and large we can accommodate whatever demand arises. There are, however, a few things to bear in mind. Some performers may have already recycled, and they simply will not be available. Others will consider a return to Earth as anti-climactic, and will turn us down. A third group may be so unknown to today's audiences that even if they were brought back from the dead, no one would care.

"Whether there will be some who will turn down a chance like this because of where the profits are going, I don't know. There could be some celebrities who would insist that some of the proceeds from their appearances go to favorite charities of their own. That sort of thing would certainly be open to negotiation, especially if the individual were someone in great demand.

"We'd expect, too, that all of these special return performances would be videotaped, and that the sales of these tapes would be substantial. We might also have certain stars do special audio and/or video tapings specifically for future marketing, and totally different from the material they used during their televised appearances.

"The possibilities are just about endless. Most performers would probably want to get their acts together while in TNW, rehearse there, then come to Earth just about ready to go on. Often, their old writers would be available to produce new scripts for these folks.

"An interesting potential difficulty comes to mind, though. What do we do about comedy teams, for instance, when one is dead and the other still alive here on Earth? The team member from TNW would be in his or her prime, while the one here on Earth would in all likelihood be over the hill. It's a puzzle, all right, but then, solving dilemmas is one of the spices of life."

With that, Hollister simply stopped talking, and waited for someone else to speak up. Not surprisingly, Bryce Wilkinson arose.

"Am I correct in assuming, Art, that you'd like Alma and me to coordinate with these four very special people, and do what we can to keep things running smoothly?"

"That's exactly right, Bryce," Hollister replied. "I have to make a few phone calls right now, and depending on what I find out, Annabelle and I will probably be on the road for a few days. Hopefully, by the time I'm back Esther will have set up an appearance for me on one of the major TV talk shows! In the meantime, everything is in your hands."

Chapter 28

On Saturday night, Hollister and Annabelle entertained Dave and Nannette Curtis for dinner, in a small private dining room in one of Madison's finest restaurants. Brad Keaton oversaw the initial serving of the meal, and arranged that extra supplies of any food or beverages the diners might require were left on a serving cart inside the room. Keaton then took up a position outside the door, to ensure that the four people inside would have complete privacy.

During dinner, Hollister filled the Curtises in on the progress his group had made, and presented each of them with inscribed and dated copies of *Fear Not The Future*. Afterward, he got down to the real purpose of the get-together.

"Dave, Nannette, it's great seeing you again. Sadly, I expect this will be the last time I see you, until sometime far in the future when we meet again in The Next World. In a few days my book will be on sale throughout most of the English-speaking world, and Annabelle and I will be traveling all over the place publicizing and promoting it. You'll probably see us on TV and read about us in the newspapers and magazines.

"We have over a hundred TNW people here on Earth right now, but most of us have to return to TNW by the end of May. Annabelle and I could stay longer, but I expect we'll go back about the time the rest of our main group does.

"By that time, we'll need a trustworthy group of Earthlings handling day-to-day printing and distribution of the book, another group operating a special non-profit foundation we'll be setting up, and a third group involved in arranging for special guest appearances of selected TNW residents who will return briefly to Earth for that purpose.

"Most important, I need someone I can trust completely, an Earthling who will oversee all the activities I've just mentioned, and see that they are staffed, managed and operated efficiently and honestly. You, Dave, are the man I want for that job. Are you interested?"

"I'm ready to help you in any way I can, Art, but what about the security considerations we talked about when you first got here last fall?"

"It may be, Dave, that we overstated those worries. At least, we haven't had any problems so far. However, I have a scheme in mind that will let you keep a very low profile and still get the job done. Every three months we'll send in a new, highly qualified, individual from TNW to be the visible boss of the operations for the ensuing three months. That person will never identify himself or herself to anyone as being from TNW. These individuals will be carefully chosen and briefed before they leave TNW, and while on Earth they will keep detailed logs of what is going on. Updates of their log entries will be provided to you each week, with copies sent to me in TNW.

"Each visible boss will take instructions directly from you, will keep you fully informed, and will reveal your identity to no one. Should you ever need to get a message to me, or vice versa, these messages will be handled by the visible bosses. How the messages are transmitted between Earth and TNW, and by whom, is about the only thing you won't know. Should you ever feel that a visible boss is incompetent, just send me a message in which you use the phrase 'truly nifty deal' somewhere in the text.

The offending party will be history very shortly after I receive such a message.

"Here's a description of the activities you'll be supervising, and a list of the names and phone numbers of Earthlings already working for our firm here, an outfit we call Totally New & Wonderful. During the next few weeks you'll be contacted by Bryce Wilkinson, Alma Norton and Howard Burns, all TNW people involved in these projects. These folks will keep you fully informed on what is going on, so when you become involved in running things you'll know what's what."

So speaking, Hollister reached into his inside suit coat pocket and withdrew two folded typewritten sheets of paper, which he handed to Curtis.

Curtis excused himself for a few minutes while he read the document. Then, nodding in agreement, Curtis shook Hollister's hand to seal their arrangement.

Soon thereafter, everyone hugged everyone, and the Curtises said good night and good-bye to Art and Annabelle.

On Sunday, Art and Annabelle drove to Chicago, checked into a hotel on Michigan Avenue, then spent the afternoon visiting the Museum of Science and Industry.

On Monday morning, shortly before 10:00, Hollister pulled his Chrysler into a parking lot adjoining a large, modern factory building on Chicago's south side. As he had expected, he had seen few buildings or other landmarks he still recognized from back in 1933 as he drove to the area. If he had it figured out correctly, the parking lot in which his vehicle now occupied a visitors' spot was located where his old factory had been. The factory building, identified by a handsome bronze plaque which said Hollister Fittings Corporation, stood on ground which Hollister recalled had formerly been occupied by two large warehouses.

Hollister, using the name Harold Arthur, had made an appointment to see Jeanne Mortenson, the company president. In the lobby, shortly before he and Annabelle reached the reception desk, Hollister noted a framed oil portrait he hadn't seen in over 60 years. The tastefully lettered brass plate below it read: "Arthur Hollister, Company Founder, 1875-1933."

Once seated in Jeanne Mortenson's office, Hollister rapidly concluded that this lady of about 47, whose grey-streaked dark brown hair set off a rather handsome face, was a serious business person first and foremost. Having noticed a wedding ring on the lady's hand, Hollister addressed her accordingly.

"Mrs. Mortenson, this is Annabelle Thompkins, but I'm not really named Harold Arthur. The problem was that if I had given your secretary my real name when I called to make an appointment, you might have had the men in white coats waiting for me when I showed up! My name is Arthur Hollister. After working for this company for about six years, I bought the firm back in 1915 and named it after myself, Hollister Plumbing Fittings. Things went pretty well, we made a bundle doing government contract work during World War I, and our business continued to expand afterward as well.

"In 1924, I sat for the portrait that now graces your lobby, and in 1933 I died in an explosion and fire in my Evanston home. For the next 60 years I resided in a place called The Next World, and during the last two of those years I wrote a book about the place. Here, by the way, is an autographed copy of that book, with my compliments."

"Mr. whoever you are," commented Mrs. Mortenson, "that's the most outlandish story I've ever heard. If it's true, you're about 120 years old now, yet you hardly look a day over 30. What conceivable proof can you supply to back-up what you've told me?

"I'm glad you asked that, Mrs. Mortenson, since proof of that nature is exactly what I'm here about. Is there someone on your security staff who is a fingerprint expert? If so, would you have him or her come to your office, with the items necessary to take and examine a set of fingerprints? Oh, by the way, if you have a notary on your payroll, please ask that party to step in here, along with whomever is your second in command."

"You're pretty good at giving orders, sir, I'll grant you that. Okay, just for the heck of it I'll play your little game. Just relax for about 10 minutes, while I make a few calls."

When the staff members whose presence Hollister had requested had assembled in Mrs. Mortenson's office, Hollister asked the security man to take a set of Hollister's fingerprints. When the prints were done, Hollister asked the security man to sign and date the card, then asked the notary to notarize the signature. Finally, Hollister asked that the oil portrait of Arthur Hollister be removed from the lobby wall and brought into the office. When that had been done, Hollister turned the portrait face-down, and asked the fingerprint man to carefully slit the cover paper along the bottom of the frame for about 18 inches, then look inside and see what he found.

After looking at Mrs. Mortenson, who nodded her approval, the security man did as instructed. After a little juggling, the man retrieved a slightly browned sheet of paper, which obviously bore a set of fingerprints. When asked, the man read aloud the name of the subject whose prints the sheet bore, and the date.

"It says Arthur Hollister, September 17, 1917," the man said.

"Okay," said Hollister, "please make a quick comparison of the two sets of prints. You should find them identical, except that the left index fingerprint on the old set will show a nasty scar across it. I injured that finger in a plant accident in 1912, when I was 38, 8 years older than this body of a 30-year-old I now inhabit more or less permanently."

The fingerprint man said that the two sets of prints seemed to match, and all present signed notarized statements as to what they had seen. In thanks, Hollister gave each person a copy of *Fear Not The Future*, and said he hoped they would enjoy reading it. When everyone else had left the office except Mrs. Mortenson, Annabelle and himself, Hollister continued his conversation with Mrs. Mortenson, who now appeared to believe what he said.

"So, Mrs. Mortenson, I imagine you're wondering how that old set of my prints came to be hidden behind my portrait. When the FBI fingerprinted all of us back in 1917, when we were engaged in war work, I asked them to make up an extra set of my fingerprints for me. They obliged, and I kept the prints in my private files for years. Then, in 1924, I sat for the portrait. When the painting was done, and the artist was ready to frame it, I asked him, on a whim, to leave the bottom edge of the backside dust cover sheet unglued. Shortly after the portrait was delivered, and before it was hung on the wall of my office, I slipped the set of prints under the cover sheet, then glued the sheet down.

"If the portrait had been lost or destroyed over the years, I'd have lost the opportunity to stage the fascinating demonstration you have just witnessed. I had already checked, and learned that the FBI periodically culls its old fingerprint files, and that their set of my prints was long gone. When your secretary told me over the phone that an oil portrait of the company founder was still on display here, I made an appointment to come and see you."

"Thanks for filling me in a bit, Mr. Hollister. But now, what else do you want from me? I have the feeling that there's more."

"For now, I'd appreciate it if you'd have your secretary make me two sets of photocopies of all the notarized statements, and of the two sets of fingerprints. Then, please keep the originals in your company safe until you hear from me again. I expect that you and your fingerprint expert will be invited to appear on a nationally televised talk show in the near future, along with Annabelle and me. You'll undoubtedly be asked to tell the audience about my visit to you, and to display the original documents. All your expenses will be paid, of course, and I'll make sure that Hollister Fittings receives a nice, tasteful plug out of all this. Believe me, I'll really appreciate your help.

"Before I go, I wonder if you can tell me a little about the company's history, after I died in 1933."

"Under the terms of your will," Jeanne Mortenson began, "the company was to be sold after your death, and the proceeds given to charity. My grandfather, Charles Lewis, was, as I'm sure you recall, the senior vice-president of the company. Grandpa managed to get sufficient backing to allow him to make the highest bid, and to purchase Hollister Plumbing Fittings outright. He saw the company through World War II, when once again there were huge profits to be made from war work.

"In 1949, 65 years old and ready for a rest, Grandpa simply turned the company over to my father, Clifton Lewis. In the early 1970's, Dad went public with the company, which became Hollister Fittings Corporation. Naturally, Dad retained a controlling stock interest. I began working here during my summer vacations from college, where my major was Business Administration, and moved into a full time position here after I graduated. When my father died in 1977, I became company president. I'm sure you'll be pleased to know that the company which bears your name continues to prosper.

"Yes, by all means, I'll do as you ask in regard to the fingerprint-related documents, and if national television calls, I will answer. It might be kind of fun!"

Having thanked Jeanne Mortenson and bid her good bye, Hollister and Annabelle bid Chicago good bye as well. Art had considered driving up through Evanston and visiting his old neighborhood, but finally decided against the idea. Instead, he simply took I-90 back towards Madison. Art was silent for a while, then spoke.

"Annabelle, there's something I've wanted to ask you about. When we both get back to TNW, how about our getting together twice a year, for a week at your place and a week at mine? Would the first week in April at your place, and the first week in October at mine work out for you?"

"That's fine with me, Art," Annabelle replied, with a smile in her voice. "We'll have a lot of shared experiences to talk about, and I'm sure there will be other ways we can amuse ourselves as well! Anyhow, I'll be at your place on the morning of October 1st."

"It's a date. And now, this being Valentine's Day, let's get back to Madison and celebrate the occasion!"

Chapter 29

Esther Fauerbach took almost no time in proving why she was one of the most highly regarded publicists in America. When she met with Hollister the next morning, Esther informed Art that beginning at 2:00 p.m. the following afternoon, his time would no longer be his own.

"It will all begin," Esther said, "with a press conference right here in Madison, in fact right here in the largest meeting room this hotel has to offer. All the major television networks will have people here, twenty-three of the country's largest newspapers will be represented, along with national and international wire services, 6 major foreign papers and, of course, the local Madison media.

"Aside from time off for meals, pit-stops and a few hours of sleep each night, you are scheduled for interviews right thru noon on Saturday. That afternoon late, eight of us fly to New York, where on Sunday evening you, Annabelle, Bryce and Alma will be guests on a one-hour CBS television special, hosted by Harry Jester.

"You'll have a rehearsal Sunday afternoon, and the show will air at 7 o'clock that night. You'll know the general format of the show by the time you go live, but the questions you'll be asked to answer will be kept secret until Harry springs them on you. Some of those questions will undoubtedly more or less duplicate ones you will already have answered for various reporters, but you can be sure some of them will be new and challenging. All four of you will answer questions, but you, as the author of *Fear Not The Future*, will probably be expected to handle the lion's share.

"Besides the four of you who are scheduled to appear on the show, I'll be going, along with Kristin Davis, who negotiated an unbelievable fee for your appearance. Brad

Keaton and Lyle Porter, our security people, will round out our group."

"You've done a great job, Esther," Hollister replied. Handing Esther a sheet of paper, Art continued. "Here's the name of the lady down in Chicago who now runs my old company. Please contact CBS, and urge them to make a spot for her and one of her employees early on in the show. It will add a bit of dramatic impact, and involve something I won't reveal at the press conference, or during any of the interviews that follow.

"The lady is named Jeanne Mortenson, and she and one of her security people, a fingerprint expert, will offer evidence that I'm the same Arthur Hollister who owned and operated her firm until his death in 1933. I'm sure the network will cover Mrs. Mortenson's expenses, but if they quibble just see Annabelle, who'll make sure that Mrs. Mortenson and her fingerprint expert receive first class treatment all the way."

"Consider that matter taken care of, Mr. Hollister. Since I have a lot of work to do, and I'm sure you do, too, I'll say good bye for now."

By the end of the week, newspaper articles about Hollister, his book, and TNW in general were appearing all over the world. Orders for Fear Not The Future were pouring in, and Leon Davis was already deluged with propositions from foreign publishers who wanted to translate the book into dozens of different languages, and sell it to the customer bases they served.

Hollister's staff was doing an excellent job, one he felt very good about as he awaited the cue which would mark the beginning of his prime time television debut. As the show opened with a long shot, Hollister sat at a grand piano, playing a medley of show tunes by George

Gershwin and Jerome Kern. After the opening credits, a voice-over announcer said: "The man playing the piano claims to be over 120 years old! His name is Arthur Hollister, and we'll meet him tonight, along with three of his fascinating friends, on this extra special show, 'A Glimpse Into The Next World!'"

By the end of this opening "teaser", the camera had zoomed in to show just the head and shoulders of a smiling Arthur Hollister, whom no one of the tens of millions of viewers would have believed looked a day over 32. After a commercial break, Harry Jester greeted the audience and introduced Arthur Hollister, Jeanne Mortenson, and Edward Narum, the fingerprint man.

"We'll get to you in a minute, Mr. Hollister," Harry Jester said, "but first I want to invite Mrs. Mortenson to tell us an interesting story."

"On the morning of February 14th of this year," Jeanne Mortenson began, "just six days ago, a man came to my office in Chicago. This man claimed to be the long dead Arthur Hollister, founder of Hollister Plumbing Fittings, predecessor to the company I now head, Hollister Fittings Corporation. My visitor, who appeared to be about 30 years old, asked me if I had someone on my security staff who was an expert on fingerprints. When I replied in the affirmative, the gentleman asked me to have my fingerprint man, along with certain other members of my staff, come to my office. Once this group was gathered, my guest asked that the fingerprint man, Mr. Narum here, take a set of his fingerprints.

"When the fingerprinting was done, my caller, whom I will refer to hereafter as Mr. Hollister, asked that a portrait of himself, then hanging in our company lobby, be brought into my office. I had that done, and now invite my security chief, Edward Narum, to tell us what happened next."

"Mr. Hollister first turned the framed portrait face down on an empty table," Narum began, "then asked me to slit the brown cover paper at the bottom of the frame, and see what I found behind it. I did so, then discovered and extracted an old set of fingerprints, dated September 17, 1917. The set of prints, which bore the official stamp of the Federal Bureau of Investigation, identified the prints as being those of an Arthur Hollister. An initial comparison of the two sets of prints showed them to be identical, except for an obvious scar on the left forefinger print of the old set. Mr. Hollister explained that the scar was the result of an injury he had sustained in 1912, when he was 38 years of age.

"Since this past Monday, I've invited the leading fingerprint experts from the Chicago Police Department and The Illinois State Crime Lab to study the two sets of prints. Both people confirmed my original opinion that the prints came from the same person, and Mrs. Mortenson now has notarized statements to that effect in her files."

"Actually," Mrs. Mortenson continued, "I have the entire file related to this matter here in this folder before me. There is not the slightest shred of evidence to indicate that this gentleman is anyone except who he claims to be, Arthur Hollister."

At this point, Harry Jester, who for a talk show host had been remarkably quiet and polite during the roughly three minutes it had taken Mrs. Mortenson and Mr. Narum to tell their stories, thanked both of them and said that after the next commercial break, he'd be back with Arthur Hollister and three of his friends, all of whom claimed to be from The Next World.

"Welcome back to 'A Glimpse Into The Next World,'" Jester began. "At this time I'd like to introduce Annabelle Thompkins, Alma Norton and Bryce Wilkinson, all friends of Art Hollister's from The Next World. Would you folks, in two or three sentences each, tell us a little about yourselves?"

"I'm Annabelle Thompkins, and I died in a train wreck back in 1898, when I was 58 years old. I've only known Art Hollister since he came back here to Earth in October of last year, but it really seems as if he and I have been friends forever."

"I'm Alma Norton, and like Art and Bryce, I died on October 6, 1933. I was a 47-year-old childless housewife when I died. My life on Earth was a good one, but I've really had more fun since I've been a resident of TNW!"

"I'm Bryce Wilkinson, and I was a prosperous Wall St. broker, age 50, when I choked to death on a piece of meat in one of New York's best restaurants. In TNW, as I did on Earth, I follow closely the football fortunes of the Wisconsin Badgers. Art Hollister is my best friend in TNW, even though he *is* a Northwestern man!"

"And now," interjected Jester, "let's have some personal background from Arthur Hollister, author of what I personally feel may become the runaway best seller of all time, *Fear Not The Future*.

"I'm Art Hollister, and I was a successful businessman in Chicago when I died at age 59. The time I've spent in TNW has been incredible! Never in my wildest dreams, while I was on Earth, could I have believed that such a wonderful, and yes, meaningful, life in the hereafter could exist. I felt that the people of Earth would be relieved and reassured to know what kind of an outlook they face after they die. That's why I wrote my book entitled *Fear Not*

The Future, and brought it here to Earth to publish, promote and distribute it."

"When we come back after the next commercial break," said Jester, "We'll go right into an extended question and answer session, with no interruptions for commercials. It should be very enlightening!"

JESTER: Art, is TNW, as you call it, a physical world, or is it more dream-like and ephemeral?
HOLLISTER: To the residents of TNW, the place seems as real as this world does to you.

JESTER: Annabelle, how and when did TNW come to be?
THOMPKINS: TNW was created during a 17-month stretch between July 1898 and December 1899. It was created by space travelers from the Planet Baldaur, working with three souls who later became known in TNW as the Great Minds. TNW opened for business on January 1, 1900. The first residents of TNW were 90 victims of a huge train wreck. Three other souls opted to take their chances under the old system, whatever that was.

JESTER: Bryce, just exactly what is TNW?
WILKINSON: It's a vast rooming house complex, with recreational facilities, and with a modicum of administration to keep things going.

JESTER: Alma, what are some of the main differences between life on Earth and Life in TNW?
NORTON: In TNW there is no crime, no hunger, no religion, no disease, no politics, no drugs, no tobacco products, no money, no envy, no pregnancy, no one under 18, no jealousy, no suffering and no marriage.

JESTER: Art, what is your position or status in TNW?
HOLLISTER: In everything but name, I'm one of the Great Minds.

JESTER: Annabelle, how is it that you met Art here on Earth rather than in TNW?
THOMPKINS: I happened to be on duty at the Earth terminal of the transport system between TNW and Earth. We met there, one thing led to another, and here I am.

JESTER: Bryce, who are the Great Minds, and what do they gain out of this?
WILKINSON: They are two brilliant men and an equally brilliant woman, who died in the same train wreck in 1898 that claimed Annabelle's life. What they get out of this is personal satisfaction, from having made things vastly better for dead souls than was ever the case before.

JESTER: Alma, this time tell us what there is in TNW, rather than what isn't.
NORTON: There's education, music, volunteer work, television, VCR's, abundant food, drink, sports, radio, books, computers, telephones, endless free new clothes, warm companionship with other souls, complete privacy for those who want it, and absolutely fantastic sex!

JESTER: Art, what will become of all the tremendous profits from the sale of your book? Evidently you can't take the money back to TNW with you.
HOLLISTER: I'll answer that question in detail just as

soon as you tell me what you do with all the money CBS pays you every year. I will say that the money will go toward funding a project which will be good for humanity, and for Planet Earth as well.

JESTER: Annabelle, in one word, how would you describe life in TNW?
THOMPKINS: Wonderful!

JESTER: Bryce, is widespread visiting of Earth by TNW residents permitted or promoted?
WILKINSON: When someone is needed for a special TNW project on Earth, volunteers are called for. Some of these people are allowed some R&R time on Earth before returning to TNW, but none gets a free pass to stay on Earth permanently. Visits to Earth simply for personal pleasure are strongly discouraged, and very seldom permitted. Those who want to return to Earth for good must recycle, and lead new lives from the very beginning.

JESTER: Alma, how many TNW residents are presently on Earth, and how long will they be here?
NORTON: Well over a hundred of us were brought in for the book publishing project, and most of us will be back in TNW by June first. There are always a few TNW people here on Earth, but their number and location are secret. I can assure you, however, that those individuals pose absolutely no threat to the Earth.

JESTER: Art, on what basis are souls accepted or rejected for residence in TNW?
HOLLISTER: Acceptance has nothing whatever to do with the individual's past religious beliefs or activities. Scum of the Earth types, plus souls which are defective

and unfit for recycling, are processed into nothingness.
Souls which have not lived at least three lifetimes on
Earth, however short those lives, must recycle
immediately. Those who have served three lifetimes or
more on Earth may recycle or not, whichever they choose.
Finally, a TNW resident may elect to recycle at any time,
or to stay in TNW forever.

JESTER: Annabelle, how is it that all of you people from
TNW look so good?
THOMPKINS: All souls entering TNW are processed by
what we know as the Wonderful Central Processor. We
enter TNW as we appeared when we were in our prime.
Those who died as infants, children or juveniles appear as
they would have, had they reached their prime. All TNW
residents then continue to look their best. They don't age.

JESTER: Bryce, are people from TNW mortal while they
are here on Earth?
WILKINSON: Yes, they are. But, should they sicken or
die from any cause while here on Earth, those individuals
are processed back to perfect condition when they return
to TNW.

JESTER: Alma, is sexual contact between Earthlings and
those from TNW forbidden, or somehow made
impossible?
NORTON: Not that I know of. I do know that all TNW
people are sterile while on Earth, just as they are in TNW.

JESTER: Art, have you ever met the soul of someone who
was a real celebrity while on Earth?
HOLLISTER: Not really. There's a pretty good comedian
named Barney Rickley living in our unit, and I think I saw

Bing Crosby once on a golf course. We all play golf as beige-colored naked souls, with our only distinctive coloring being the decorations on our golf hats, so I can't really be sure it was Bing.

JESTER: Annabelle, can you feel pain or pleasure in TNW?
THOMPKINS: You can't feel physical pain, but there are times you can feel the emotional variety. You can laugh, you can cry. You can feel immense pleasure, whether it's from sex, other pleasant social activities, personal accomplishment or just the delightful fragrance of a flower or a fine perfume.

JESTER: Bryce, do you have any awareness of the passage of time, and of what is going on here on Earth, while you're in TNW?
WILKINSON: Yes. Our time is the same as that on Earth, and we use the same calendars that Earthlings do. We're painfully aware of the goings on here on Earth—the wars, political squabbles and all the rest. Sometimes it all makes us laugh, more often it makes us want to cry.

JESTER: Alma, can a soul be booted out of TNW for misconduct?
NORTON: Not that I know of.

JESTER: Finally, Art, are there any additional projects you intend to tackle once you get back to TNW?
HOLLISTER: As a matter of fact there are. In TNW, I think we should encourage more residents to write books, articles, plays, short stories and poetry, for distribution to other TNW souls. These things could be printed, or

passed along by electronic data equipment—that is, by computer, FAX, CD Rom, floppy disks or what have you. As regards our continued contact with Earth, we already have plans to set up return engagements on Earth by various now dead celebrities from the entertainment, political and sports worlds. Electronic mail between Earth and TNW may also be established in the not too distant future. The possibilities are incredible, and we'll be pursuing them.

"Thank you all very much," said Harry Jester. "I may take part in a more exciting television presentation sometime, but somehow I doubt it.

"Once more, and I admit this is an out and out plug, the book to look for, Art Hollister's story of The Next World, is entitled *Fear Not The Future*."

Chapter 30

It was May 25, 1994. Nearly all TNW people involved in the book project had gone back to TNW. Book sales were booming, and the Special Celebrity Visit To Earth program was off to an excellent start. Money was pouring into the coffers of The World Population Studies Foundation. From a safe distance, masked by a straw boss from TNW, David Curtis was doing a superb job, keeping everything running smoothly.

On this beautiful spring day, Hollister and Annabelle were in Minneapolis. Annabelle was the special guest on a local TV show, accompanied by Lyle Porter as her body guard.

Art, escorted by the ever-faithful Brad Keaton, was autographing books at a major book outlet. In the two hours he'd been there, Hollister thought, he must have signed 100 copies, and there still seemed to be about 40 more people waiting in line. Thankfully, Hollister reflected that the next day, at The Mall of America in Bloomington, he'd be undergoing an ordeal like this for the last time.

Handing a book back to a lady, Hollister turned to his next customer. The man almost threw a book at him. Then in an odd, almost choked voice, he spoke. "Mr. Hollister, my name is Charles Anderson. For years I've run a small publishing company, printing religious tracts and little comic booklets, pushing doomsday and similar themes. Stuff to scare the kiddies in Sunday Schools, and get their parents worrying, too. It was a great racket until you came along, with the love and happiness message of your Next World. You've screwed up my livelihood, and you're going to pay for it!"

Realizing he was in danger, Hollister dropped his pen and attempted to draw his Beretta. Before Hollister's gun cleared leather, Anderson had pumped three rounds from a snub-nosed .38 into Hollister's chest. As Hollister slumped over dead, Anderson plowed through the crowd, heading for the outside door. Brad Keaton let Anderson take five steps, and break into the clear, before he put two 9 mm. rounds into the 10 ring, nearly separating Anderson's head from his body.

Arthur Hollister rubbed his eyes and looked around him. He was in the Receiving Area of TNW's Central Processing, once more a naked soul among other naked souls. Hollister wondered idly how long it would take before he got back to Unit 414, and could call a special meeting of the Frolicsome Four.

THE END